Tales from the Storm

Omnibus

C.R. Langille

Praise for C.R. Langille

"C.R. Langille's collection, *Tales from the Storm: Volume One* succeeds at showcasing his ability to write horror." -Daniel Yocom of Guild Master Gaming

"*Tales From the Storm* is a unique collection of short horror stories that just might make you squirm." -Jasmine, Goodreads

"In this collection of short fiction, he excels at bringing the horror, suspense, and the supernatural into a macabre play of action and intent." -K. Scott Forman author of *Lovecraft's Pillow*

"Langille's ability to write vivid imagery means that this dark fantasy doesn't shy away from wading into some pretty horrific waters. I realize that it's cliche to say that I could see the scenes like a movie in my head, but in this case, I embrace the stereotype. " Review of *Canyon Shadows*, -J.L. Gribble, author of the *Steel Empires Series*

"This is the first book I've read by this author. If you like Stephen King, you will LOVE this. From the first sentence I was addicted. I couldn't put it down." Review of *Consequence*, -Lisa B., Amazon

Tales from the Storm: A Collection of Horror Stories

Omnibus

by C.R. Langille

Copyright © 2022, C.R. Langille

Published by Timber Ghost Press

Printed in the United States of America

Edited by: Beverly Bernard

Cover Art and Design by: Don Noble of Rooster Republic Press

Interior Design: Timber Ghost Press

Print ISBN: 979-8-9855521-5-7

Contents

Foreword

This collection represents a special thing for me because many of these stories are my first publishing successes. For an author, that first accepted story marks a milestone. For me, that story was "The Scratch" which appeared in *Dark Moon Books Presents: Ghosts!*

Funny thing about that story, it was inspired partly by true events. I had traveled to Denver, Colorado on business and when I went to my hotel room after checking in, every drawer and cupboard was open. I think I started drafting the story that night.

Writing short stories is one of my preferred mediums. I like them because they are each so unique and offer an avenue to direct my creativity. I also find them challenging. With a short story you don't have as much time to develop characters or plots. Everything has to be precise; each word counts and there isn't room to let the story wander.

I hope you enjoy this collection as much as I enjoyed writing each story.

-Cody

For fans of horror.

"The Spot"

G rey clouds the color of wet ash grumbled across the afternoon sky in a slow shuffle. Thunder boomed in the distance. Graham's buckskin let out a shrill whinny, but he patted the horse's neck until it calmed.

The dull clouds contrasted with the bright colors of the leaves. Pockets of pumpkin orange, warm buttery yellow, and blood red dotted the mountainside.

Graham navigated to the side of the road and waited for Emmett to catch up. Two older plow horses pulled an old Ford pick-up bed which Emmett turned into a wagon. With every bump and rock in the road, the old wagon screamed something violent.

"How much longer," Graham asked.

"Another hour or so. No need to piss your britches," Emmett said.

The wagon squeaked by, and the Emmett pulled a tattered wool scarf down from his face to reveal a beard the same color as the storm-laden sky. The old man spit a wad of tobacco in Graham's general direction before he adjusted his wide brim hat and shot him a toothless smile.

Graham returned the smile and adjusted his coat. With summer gone, the air had turned crisp and cold. He was thankful that Theresa had fixed up his wool coat before he left. Graham hoped that she would be okay while he was gone. It was only a week, but a week was too much. They were engaged and planned to marry when he returned.

He rode ahead to escape the squeak and squeal of Emmett's wagon. After a moment, the wagon's cry faded into the background and only the clip-clop of his horse's hooves on the broken asphalt graced his ears. A large building made of brick stood at a T intersection in the road. All the windows were broken, and an ivy plant crawled up the front of the dilapidated structure and covered it like moss on a log. Like everything else in the city, the only residents were half-forgotten memories, and dust—lots and lots of dust.

A young horse with a black leather saddle was hitched to an old gas pump and snorted when it saw Graham. Graham cursed under his breath and nudged his buckskin into a gallop. They weren't supposed to enter the buildings alone. As he neared the building he cupped his hands and bellowed.

"Randall! You there?"

His voice echoed through the building and caused a nearby murder of crows to take flight. They cawed their annoyance as they flew away.

"Randall, stop messing around," Graham said.

Graham tightened his grip on the reins until his knuckles were whiter than the nearby snow-capped peaks. He steered the horse next to Randall's and hopped off. The building stared at him with murderous intent. The town elder told them all stories of what some unsuspecting child would find in the dark and blasted buildings of the city.

"Randall?"

Graham's voiced cracked ever so slightly as doubt crept into his spine. He wanted to just leave him be and let Fate decide what she had in store for the boy. Graham had known the boy would be trouble the moment they started training together. But, he couldn't bring himself to leave Randall behind. Besides, it would mean longer shifts during the watch without him.

"Savior's light, Randall, come out, please!"

Graham took a step toward the building but stopped when the sound of brick against concrete scraped from inside. The tell-tale squeak of Emmett's wagon bolstered his confidence, but not by much. The wind picked up and carried the fetid stench of the Dead Lake to his nose. The lake was supposedly saltier than the vast oceans Graham heard about but never seen. The Dead Lake was impressive, but the stink reminded him of chicken eggs gone rotten. Some folk told stories, saying they saw all sorts of fancy things near and in the lake. The most common tale was that something big lived underneath the briny water, and if you watched on a blood moon, you could see its colossal body roll beneath the moonlight. But those were just tales.

"He in there?" Emmett asked.

Graham nodded and kept his eyes glued to the building. A shadow flitted across the ivy-covered doorway.

"Randall! Come on out, we've got miles yet to go, boy!" Emmett said.

The old man's voice was barely more than a wheeze on the wind. Graham dismounted his horse and hitched the reins to the same gas pump as Randall's. He started toward the building when Emmett whistled from behind.

Graham turned just in time to catch a worn tomahawk.

"You've got five minutes, boy. Then I'm leaving. At least one of us needs to take the watch."

Graham nodded and tightened his grip on the weapon. It wasn't much and had seen better days, but it was better than nothing.

"Five minutes," Emmett reiterated.

The old man lit a pipe and looked to the sky. It was getting late, and the rain would fall at any moment. If they didn't make it to their destination before the rain, it would be miserably cold.

Graham stepped through the ivy gateway and into the building. There was a different smell inside. Unlike the dry, dust-strewn scent of the valley, the building was musty and wet. This gas station was bigger than others he'd seen, and surrounded by an empty sea of asphalt. Emmett said it used to be a truck stop.

The odd drip-drip-drip of water echoed through the empty shell and played at Graham's nerves. It sounded too much like one of the big grand-daddy clocks he'd seen in the town square, constantly ticking until it drove a man insane.

"Randall," Graham said as loud as he dared. His words raced through the old pump station until they returned to him, out of breath.

The inside of the building was just as decrepit and time-worn as the outside. The drip-drip-drip of the water lulled Graham in further.

"You there? Come on out! We got to get on down the road or we're going to get rained on!" Graham said, a little louder this time.

The drips stopped, and so did Graham. There was a scrape of metal against brick from further in the building and something moved through the shadows.

"Randall?"

The sound of tearing fabric crept through the room and up Graham's spine. He wanted to turn tail and run, but he didn't want to leave Randall behind.

The tearing stopped and then there was a splash of water. Then a giggle. Then nothing.

"Randall?" Graham asked.

He took a couple of nervous steps toward the shadows. That's when the whispers caressed his ears. Graham couldn't tell what the voice was saying, but it made him want to throw up. When he looked up, he was just at the shadow's edge, and he didn't remember walking so close to the darkness.

Randall was crouched in front of him, poking the water with an old branch. The drip-drip-drip echoed through the room, but Graham couldn't see where the noise came from.

"Randall?" Graham said.

The boy kept his back turned toward Graham and continued to poke the water's edge.

"Come on now, we have to get a move on," Graham said.

The whispers picked up in intensity, and his vision blurred for a moment. He almost caught a word or two in the insane murmurs. Randall continued to poke at the water, so Graham reached down and shook the boy's shoulder. All at once the whispers stopped and the drip-drip-drip died away.

Randall dropped the stick and turned toward Graham. The boy's face was pale and covered in sweat. Randall's eyes were glazed over and unfocused, but when Graham shook him once more, the boy's eyes found their clarity and snapped on Graham.

"Graham?" Randall asked.

"Yeah, it's me. Come on. Emmett is waiting on us."

Randall looked around and stood.

"Where are we?" Randall asked.

"An old fill'em'up station. Come on."

The village elders warned them not to go playing around in the old building by themselves. Strange things happen when the living step foot in a dead building they said. Strange things. They were probably just stories to scare children, but Graham was starting to think perhaps there was a smidgen of truth to the tall tales.

Graham started to lead Randall out, hoping that some fresh air would do the boy some good. It wouldn't do if they had to babysit Randall and watch the spot. Maybe they could send the boy back with the other team if he was still in a stupor.

As they turned to leave, Randall threw the stick into the darkened room. It hit the water and sank without a sound.

Emmett was in the process of turning the wagon around when they stepped outside. Graham's ears popped as if he had just come off the mountain and into the valley. The fresh air, while tinged with the Dead Lake's stench, still felt nice across his cheeks.

Emmett noticed the pair and stopped the wagon. He motioned them over with a free hand. Graham helped Randall over to the wagon, but with each step, it seemed the boy got his strength back. By the time they reached Emmett, Randall was walking unassisted. The pair stopped short when Emmett leveled a sawed-off shotgun toward their faces.

"Let me see," he said.

"I'm fine, Emmett. I promise," Randall said.

"Quit your bellyaching. It's your fault anyway," Graham said.

Graham slapped Randall across the back of the head and inched as close as he dared to Emmett. The shotgun followed his movement and didn't waver a bit. When he couldn't get any closer, Graham held an eyelid open with his fingers and rolled his eye around in the socket, exposing all the whites to the old man. Then, he followed suit with the other eye.

Emmett nodded and then motioned Graham to the side before he aimed the gun back at Randall.

"Come on, boy. Your turn," Emmett said.

"This is ridiculous! Ain't nothing happened in that old building. I swear," Randall said.

The old man pulled the hammers back on the shotgun.

"I could blast you right now and be within my rights. Better safe than sorry, you know. Plus, you'd rather die this way than if you're infected," the old man said.

Randall looked to Graham for support, but Graham only motioned him toward Emmett. The old man was right if Randall was infected, better to die by being shot than let the infection run its course. Safer for everyone involved.

The boy sighed and stepped closer. He opened one eye, then the other.

"There, just like I told you, no infection."

Emmett eased the hammers back into place on the gun. Then he pulled his scarf up over his mouth and started the wagon rolling again with the whip of the reins.

Graham kicked his horse into motion and pushed past the wagon. He made sure Randall stayed between him and Emmett, and constantly checked back to ensure the boy didn't wander off again. Randall didn't pay as much attention to their training, and it was showing now.

As they made their way through the abandoned city, the ambient noise of life died away. The birds no longer chirped, and the bugs no longer buzzed. It was as if the city itself had stopped breathing. Off in the distance, a giant sinkhole pock-marked the city. Even at a distance, the hole seemed massive as it stretched across several city blocks. The towns-folk who had been out this far, nicknamed it The Pit. Some people came back telling stories of strange orange lights that danced in the pit during the witching hour. Graham was just happy that they weren't going anywhere near the thing. Their destination was something else, something more important than abandoned holes.

The temperature dropped as they navigated through empty streets. The remnants of cars and trucks lay in rusted heaps along the road. Others had cleared a path to their destination long before Graham had been born. Randall looked down the side streets, and it was easy enough to tell that travel with the wagon would have been impossible otherwise.

They moved closer to their destination. The sun began to set behind the mountains and cast the evening sky with a darker gloom. Graham's father used to talk about the mag-nificent Fall sunsets that would light up the heavens. Graham supposed there was a lot of beauty in the world back before.

They rounded the corner to find kerosene torches lining the sidewalks on either side of the road. The flames in each torch were steady and danced in what little breeze there was. The squeak of Emmett's wagon told him the old man was close, and that's when Graham noticed he had stopped his horse at the edge of the torches.

The light from each torch cut through the shadows and provided enough illumination to the keep the street lit in the darkness. The torches led the way and ended near a large building. An asphalt lot full of rusted and empty cars stood between them and a hotel—their destination.

The hotel was five stories tall. Dozens of windows lined the outer wall facing them. Most of the windows were broken, and the wind moved tattered curtains making it look as if people moved about and watched them from darkened rooms. A wagon, similar to Emmett's, was stationed out front, with a team of horses hitched nearby.

Emmett brought the wagon to a stop next to the two and then climbed down. The old man let out a groan and popped his back.

"Getting too old for these trips. I think this will be my last one boys," he said. "You wait here. If I don't come back, you know what to do."

Emmett double-checked to make sure the shotgun was loaded, then walked down the street. Graham watched him go until the old man disappeared into the hotel. Working the fields started to look like it was perhaps the better option. Theresa didn't want him to come on this trip, and she had said they could wait for him to make enough chits in the fields. Graham didn't want to wait, though.

"What do we do if he doesn't come back?" Randall asked.

Graham sighed and turned his attention to the younger man. Hadn't the boy listened during the training? It had been a mistake to bring two new watchers on the trip, but at least

Graham had excelled during the instruction—much to Theresa's chagrin.

"If he doesn't come back, then we go in after him. We can't leave the watch unattended for any reason."

"But what if something killed him, or he's infected?' Randall asked.

"Any reason," Graham replied, and turned his gaze back to the house. He checked his belt for the tomahawk Emmett had given him and found comfort in its weight.

He didn't have a watch, so he was unsure of how long the old man was gone. Graham was about to head in when Emmett appeared at the doorway of the abandoned house. The old man stepped out into the street and headed back to the wagon.

"Everything okay?" Graham asked.

The old man shot him a look. The cold sentiment behind Emmett's eyes said everything. Graham lowered his head.

"All of them?" Graham asked.

"Almost."

"What? What's wrong?" Randall asked.

A slight tremor shook the boy's words. It was definitely a bad idea to bring him along. Why did the town council allow such a green crew to accompany the old man on the trip?

"They lost two," Emmett said.

Graham stopped. Two, dead. They hadn't lost a person in more than three seasons, and now they just lost two.

Emmett whipped the reins and sent the wagon moving again. A moment later, Graham and Randall followed behind.

They entered through the front of the hotel. The original doors, long broken and gone, were replaced with heavy wooden ones. The doors screamed and creaked when opened and Graham flinched as the noise echoed down the street.

"Don't worry, sound doesn't attract anything here. Not anymore at least," Emmett said.

Warm air caressed Graham's cold face as he stepped over the threshold. It came as such a shock he stopped and looked around. It wasn't just the warmth of being indoors, it was something else. The air inside was humid and heavy, not what he was used to in the arid mountains.

"I don't like it in here," Randall said.

Graham shared the boy's sentiments but kept his mouth shut. Emmett ushered them into the lobby where empty boxes of supplies sat in various states of disarray. The old man pointed to a corner.

"Bring our stuff and put it there," Emmett said.

Graham nodded and turned to Randall. Emmett walked down the hall and disappeared.

"Let's get it done," Graham said.

They spent the next ten minutes unloading the wagon. As they brought the last load into the lobby, Emmett returned with another man. Graham recognized the man from the village; it was Bartholomew, the town's apprentice blacksmith. He was older than Graham and Randall, but younger than Emmett. Bartholomew wore a long, stringy beard on his face. For some reason, the man still had on his heavy leather blacksmithing apron and carried a large steel hammer which glistened red in the flickering candlelight.

"You should stay until morning, a storm's coming," Emmett said.

Bartholomew didn't say anything at first. He just stared at the ground with his hand gripping the hammer so hard his knuckles turned white.

"Can't stay here anymore," Bartholomew said.

Emmett didn't say anything. He clapped Bartholomew's shoulder once, then turned toward us.

"Help him bring up the others," Emmett said.

Bartholomew didn't go with them, merely pointed in the direction they needed to go. Emmett sighed and led them to the stairwell.

"Go down the stairs and take a right when you exit. You'll see it. We need to hurry this up because we can't leave the spot unattended for too much longer. Don't you boys go looking at it either, not until it's your shift. You hear me?"

"Okay," Graham said.

Randall didn't respond, seemed lost in the darkness of the stairwell, like when he was at the gas station earlier. They shouldn't have brought the boy.

"Randall!" Emmett said. "You understand?"

"Yes, sir," Randall said.

"Good. Now go."

They walked down and their footfalls echoed through the stairwell. There were more candles and torches lining the walls, but the further down the stairs they went, the darker it became. The humidity increased, and by the time they arrived in the basement, Graham wanted to pull his coat off.

Graham turned right as they went through the doors, not only because it was the way Emmett told him to go, it was the only way to go. The floors above had caved in years ago and blocked off any other direction.

Skeletons of the dead and forgotten were trapped within the rubble. Graham wondered why nobody had ever dug them out and gave them proper burials, but as he got closer to the pile of debris, he understood. A sense of utter sadness rolled through his guts, and he lost the will to do anything. Despair crawled through his body and doused his insides with and icy cold that had a bite much more bitter than the mountain streams. Lost in the cloud of depression, Graham thought of Theresa. She was right—he should never have come here. The infection would burrow into his body, then they would never be together, or worse he would carry the infection back to her.

He wanted to leave, and go back to Theresa, but they'd come this far and he had a duty to uphold now. Graham sighed.

"Come on," Graham said.

They entered the room to the right of the stairs.

It was an old laundry room. Graham recognized the giant machines from the stories his parents had told him. They talked about the machines with a sense of longing. Candles lined every flat surface other than the floor. The dance of candlelight was nearly maddening as the light and shadow constantly played tag along the walls.

A large, grimy white sheet, held up by heavy duty rope, cut the room into two sections. Graham knew that the spot was one the other side of the sheet. The spot they were supposed to watch when it was their time.

Randall pointed to the corner by one of the washing machines. Two bodies wrapped in the same dirty linen as the hanging sheet lay on the floor. Graham didn't know who the two were, and he didn't want to know.

They went to work and hauled the first body up the stairs. Sweat poured down Graham's face and stung his eyes as he ascended the stairs, and the cool autumn air kissed his skin as they carried the body to Bartholomew's wagon. The chill air was a nice relief, and he didn't want to go back for the second body, but he knew Emmett would get after them for dilly-dallying.

The blacksmith was in the wagon and ready by the time they loaded the second body into the rusted truck bed. Bartholomew cracked the reins and set the wagon into motion. Somehow, his wagon was even squeakier than Emmett's.

After they unpacked all the supplies, Emmett walked up with three small sticks in his hand. He held the three sticks so that they appeared to be the same length, although Graham knew that one of them would be shorter than the other two.

"Go on, pull a stick."

Graham reached out and pulled one. He didn't have to see the other sticks to know the truth—he would be first.

Emmett led Graham down the stairs. Neither of them said a word until they arrived at the room. The sheet still split the room into two halves, but this time, everything seemed a little darker, and Graham hesitated at room's threshold.

Emmett handed Graham a pack full of supplies and placed a hand on his shoulder.

"Remember, you don't have to watch it all the time. Just make sure to keep an eye on it at least once or twice an hour," Emmett said.

Graham nodded. This would be his first watch. They trained him, but this was the real deal.

"If it grows bigger, you come get us, okay?"

"Okay."

Emmett started up the stairs but called back down.

"Randall will be down to relieve you in eight hours," Emmett said. "Don't fall asleep."

Don't fall asleep. Graham didn't think it would be a problem. The room made his skin crawl, and there was a horrible sense of someone watching him. Graham wished he had more than the old tomahawk with him. Emmett was the only one with a gun. The elders didn't give out many guns due to the ammo shortage. Besides, the last time anyone used a gun on watch was years ago. What good would a gun do against the spot?

Graham stepped up next to the sheet and reached out to pull the cloth aside with a shaky hand. He took a deep breath to steady himself, then opened the curtain and stepped on through to the other side.

A plain wooden chair sat in the middle of the room facing a wall of red brick. The wall was undecorated and in a poor state of health. A large crack started at the floor and branched off into three different directions, but that wasn't the most significant feature of the wall.

In the middle of the brick wall, was a dark spot, blacker than Emmett's coffee, and no bigger than the size of one of

Theresa's red apples. Other than some lit candles, an old tape measure, a wind-up clock, and a pad of paper, nothing else was in the room. At least, nothing Graham could see.

He still couldn't shake the feeling that someone or something watched him. There wasn't anyone else, though, at least not on that side of the sheet.

Graham set his supplies down and picked up the notebook. Each page was full of dates, times, and measurements. Occasionally there were observations or unreadable scribbles. Graham flipped to the last page with writing on it. The final entry was logged two hours ago. It read: *Sunday, Hour 19, 2 & 1/4 inches.*

He put the notebook down and picked up the tape measure. Graham took a couple of steps toward the spot but stopped short. He didn't want to go near it. Theresa told him not to touch it. She said that he would definitely become infected. Graham wasn't sure if that was the truth, and in his training, they didn't confirm or deny that aspect. However, they did say not to touch it if it could be avoided.

Graham pulled a length of tape from the measure. The old device groaned and squealed as he pulled. Then, he held it up next to the spot and looked. 2 & 1/2 inches. It had grown.

He almost dropped the tape measure and ran back up the stairs, but he stopped himself. The training took over. Three times, his instructor said. Always measure three times for an accurate reading.

Graham held the measure up again. 2 & 1/4. He held his breath and held it up one more time. 2 & 3/8. Graham let the air rush from his lungs in a contented sigh. While the measurement was larger than the previous entry, it didn't meet the threshold for growth. His instructor said there would be human error, and not to worry if the measurement was off by a couple sixteenths.

He returned to the chair and wound up the clock. It would ring an alarm in two hours and would notify him it was time to measure the spot again. Until then, he just had to keep an eye on it, and not fall asleep.

Graham watched the wall, focused on the inky blotch. It seemed to move under the candlelight as if it ate the light itself. He resisted the urge to measure it again, even though it looked somewhat bigger. Only when the alarm sounds, that's what they said in his training. It would still be over an hour before the alarm—

The bells of the clock started to ring and Graham almost fell out of the chair. It couldn't be time yet, he'd just set the danged thing. Yet, when he looked down, the clock read true. It had been two hours. The state of the candles confirmed his suspicion, as they had burned lower.

He measured the spot again. 2 & 3/8, 2 & 7/16, 2 & 7/16. It was larger than before, but not by enough to worry. Graham set the clock once again and took care to ensure he did it correctly. He grabbed his bag of supplies and looked for something to eat.

The bag held the usual rations, enough to get someone by for eight hours: half a loaf of bread, some cheese, and a sack of jerky. He also had his waterskin, and it was at that moment he realized just how thirsty he was.

Graham lifted the skin up to his lips and tipped it back, but nothing came out. He tipped it back further, but still, empty. It wasn't right. He wasn't a rookie when it came to the outdoors, and he knew what a full waterskin felt like versus an empty one; this one was heavy enough to be half full. Theresa always reminded him to keep it half full, because she didn't want him dying of thirst out in the fields.

Graham lifted it to his lips once again, but nothing came out. He growled and tipped it over, and was surprised when all the liquid gushed out onto the concrete floor. Graham just stared at the water, unsure of what to think. His instructor at training said the spot would play tricks on him. That it would try to get him to fall asleep or leave. That's all this was, was a trick—a costly trick, but a trick nonetheless.

"Emmett! Randall! Can you hear me?"

Nothing but silence. In fact, the air was thicker than before. His shouts were muted and Graham knew the others wouldn't hear him. He would just have to wait it out. It was only six more hours, and Randall would take over. Graham could wait six hours.

The fields were starting to look like a good option at this point. Theresa would understand. She'd probably be happy with his choice. The fields were hard work, and had their own dangers, but nothing like the watch. Most people didn't last too many seasons on watch. The majority quit and returned to the fields, while others ended up like the Bartholomew's teammates, or insane.

Graham looked at the clock, and his face scrunched up with confusion. He picked it up and listened to ensure the tick-tock of the internal mechanism still sounded. Then, he watched to make sure the hands still moved as they were supposed to move. Everything looked to be in order, which was why he couldn't fathom that it had only been one minute since he set it last.

"I'm here," Randall said.

Graham let out a scream and dropped the clock. It hit the ground and the alarm sent the bells ringing.

"Savior's light, you scared me," Graham said.

His breath came in ragged waves and it felt as if his heart would stop at any moment. Randall just smiled and let out a little laugh.

"Sorry. How's it going?" Randall asked.

"Strange. I swear I've lost time down here. I've only measured the spot twice."

Randall's smile disappeared and he picked up the notebook. The boy stared at the water for a moment.

"What's with the puddle?" Randall asked.

"I spilled my water," Graham said.

He didn't want to explain what happened. It would only make the boy nervous.

"According to this, you met all your measurements," Randall said.

Impossible. He'd only measured twice.

"Give me that."

Graham took the book from him and opened it to the last entry. He wanted to leave. He wanted to get on his horse and go back to the village. As Randall stated, all the measurements were filled out, and in Graham's handwriting. He didn't remember taking the measurements, or writing anything down. Graham had trouble recalling anything past the waterskin incident. He turned the page almost dropped the book. Written in his handwriting was the following sentence over, and over: *Plant Theresa in the fields, then see what the harvest yields.*

There was the wet sound of tearing. Graham had heard the same sound when the hunters would skin out their game. Both Graham and Randall looked to the spot, and for just a moment, it seemed as if the entire wall fluttered like it was paper in the wind. The tearing sounded again and Graham took a step back. Then, it stopped, and the wall no longer shuddered. The candlelight brightened and only then did Graham realize just how dark it had been.

"What the hell's going on down here," Emmett asked as he entered the room.

Graham took the opportunity to rip the notebook page out and stuff it in his pocket before Emmett crossed through the linen sheet. The old man had the gun in hand again.

"Graham's been infected. He's going crazy," Randall said.

Graham's jaw dropped and he turned to the boy.

"That's insane! I'm fine," he said.

Emmett leveled the shotgun and motioned for Graham to take a seat. Graham wanted to argue, but the look in Emmett's eyes stopped that notion. He took a seat.

Emmett stood over him with the gun poised and ready.

"Open 'em," the old man said.

Graham followed the order and held his eyes open to let Emmett inspect them. After a moment, Emmett sighed and lowered the weapon.

"He's fine. We don't have to plant him in the fields," Emmett said.

Plant Theresa in the fields, then see what the harvest yields.

"What did you say?" Graham asked.

"I said you're fine. Well, at least you're not infected. Go get some sleep. The watch can take a lot out of you."

Graham nodded. Sleep sounded like a fine idea, as well as a drink of water. He glanced down at the puddle and frowned. Ripples rolled across the small puddle, and for a moment, the dark depths seemed to go down forever. Emmett gave him a slight shake on the shoulder and motioned for him to go.

"I'll make sure Randall is set up for his watch, then I'll be up," Emmett said.

"Okay."

Graham walked up the stairs. With each step, he could breathe easier, and an invisible weight seemed to slip off his shoulders. He walked outside and the night air felt good in his lungs. The sun would be up soon, and hopefully with it, the light would bring some warmth.

Graham ate some food outside with the horses. They smelled of hard work and purpose and reminded him of the village. Of the fields. *....see what the harvest yields.* Of Theresa.

He finished his dinner and returned to the lobby. Emmett or Randall must have set up the cots, but it didn't matter who did, only that he had a decent place to sleep. Graham crawled onto the cot. The stress and pull of travel melted away as he settled in for the night. Then, he fell asleep.

The sound of a shotgun blast ripped Graham from his slumber. He sat up and groaned as his road-weary muscles protested.

The sun was out, and given the way, the light poured through the window, was almost setting again. Graham tried to determine just how long he had slept when another shotgun blast echoed from the basement. He sprang up and ran down the stairs. Graham slowed as he neared the debris pile and the entrance to the room.

Emmett hummed a tune which carried out into the stairwell. Graham put his body against the wall and peeked into the room. The sheet was up and obscured his vision, but he could still see the hunched over shadow of Emmett as he reloaded the shotgun. Randall was on the floor, with only his hand visible from outside the white cloth. Graham contemplated sneaking back up the stairs. He could get on his horse and be back to the village in a day if he rode hard.

"He was infected," Emmett said.

Graham froze.

"I had to put him down. It was the right thing to do. You know that, right?"

Graham took a deep breath and stepped across the threshold. The metallic taste of blood permeated the room and he almost gagged.

"I had to. We can plant him in the fields when we get home," Emmett said.

Graham walked slowly toward the white sheet. He reached out and grabbed onto the fabric and flinched when his hand contacted something warm and wet on the linen.

"How about you put the gun down, Emmett," Graham said.

The old man started humming again as Graham pulled the sheet to the side. The room was empty and the humming stopped mid-tune. Randall was gone, Emmett was gone. The old man's shotgun was on the ground.

Blood covered the floor, and there was a distinct path showing where someone dragged a body across the floor toward the brick wall. There was the sound of water dripping into a puddle, but the water on the floor was still as a pane of glass. That wasn't what held Graham's attention. The spot on the wall had grown. The black splotch covered the entire brick wall in a substance that reminded him of tar. It pulsed as if breathing, and small, inky tendrils crawled toward the blood on the concrete.

Graham turned to run and found Emmett and Randall standing behind him. They stared past him with eyes the color of burnt coals. He took a step back into the room but stopped when something brushed across his leg. It was cold and wet and promised him horrible things.

About the story: "The Spot" originally appeared in *Weird-book #35*, published by Wildside Press in May of 2017. It's one of my favorite short stories because I think it really taps into that slow kind of horror that gets under your skin. It was kind of a hard sell and I sent it to a number of publishers before Wildside picked it up. I think it found a lovely home with Weirdbook though, because it is definitely a weird tale. If you've read my book, *Consequence*, then you might have caught some references... perhaps a little background as to what may have caused the spot to appear.

"Brine & Blood"

S tories like these usually start with bad weather, which would account for the deluge attacking the Salt Lake Valley. We don't get a lot of rain in Utah in the summer months, and when we do, it's usually over before you could say, it's raining. This storm, however, was different. It started two days ago and it hadn't stopped.

The raindrops hit my windshield loud enough to drown out the traffic update on the radio. The update wasn't necessary though; the sea of red lights in front of me mirrored by the Soviet bread-line of vehicles on the other side of the highway was update enough. I was a creature of habit though, and getting the daily traffic was more ritual than anything.

The ritual was shattered when the call came in on my cell phone. Holly, my secretary, had me install a nice Bluetooth system so I wouldn't have to mess with the phone. Something about hands-free being safer or some bullshit.

"This is Morgan," I said.

"Hey, Boss, I've got a woman here. Says she has a job for you."

It was Holly. She had a meek voice, almost a whisper. Yet, once you tuned your ear to it, it came in crystal clear. Caused problems sometimes on the phone with clients, but she had a way with organization that would impress any Wall Street tycoon.

"Stuck in traffic, Hon. Going to be another twenty minutes until I get back."

"The woman says she'll wait," Holly said. "Oh, and Boss?"

"Shoot."

"Don't call me hon. We've talked about it before."

I chuckled. She had a quiet bark to her and I liked the fire. Besides, it was a game we played and I was sure she enjoyed it as much as I did.

Thirty minutes later, I pulled into the parking lot of my small office. The office of Bartholomew Morgan, Private Investigations was sandwiched between a Dollar Tree and a Great Clips in the middle of West Valley City. We had an advertisement in the phone book, but Holly was quick to tell me that we needed an online presence as well. I wasn't so sure, but when we only had just enough clients to pay the bills (during good months), I relented. Taking care of the site was one of her additional duties.

Even with the influx of clients from the website, times were getting tough. We had been late on rent last month, and if this job didn't go through, we'd be kicked out before the end of the next month.

The door squealed as I walked in, and Holly shuddered. She stood up, grabbed a can of WD-40 from her desk, and marched over as I was hanging my hat on the coat rack.

"When are you going to get this fixed? I have to spray this thing at least twice a day," she said.

"Why do I need to fix it if you keep it working, Hon?"

She shot me a glare over the rims of her tortoise shell glasses. The look said the next time I said the word, Hon, she'd spray *me* in the face with the WD-40 instead of the squeaky hinges.

"Your potential new client is in your office. Ms. Whatley is her name."

"Why did you let her back there?"

Holly shot me a smile. It was payback. She knew I didn't like clients poking around in my office when I wasn't there.

"Touché."

I opened the door to my office and it was surprisingly quiet. The subtle odor of lubricant told me Holly had already hit these hinges. However, it wasn't the audible state of the door that caught my attention, it was Ms. Whatley.

She had her back to me, but I could already tell that she was a looker. She wore a summer dress that was short enough to leave little to my imagination (and I have a big imagination). Long hair the color of coffee was pulled into a tight bun. The hint of a tattoo on the nape of her neck was visible; not enough to tell what it was, but enough that I knew I wanted to see more.

She turned to face me and caught me with the biggest blue eyes I'd ever seen. They were light blue like a pure glacier and contrasted with her dark hair in the most dramatic way.

She stood up and extended a hand. I shook it, careful to find that perfect grip, not too strong, but not too weak to be demeaning. The scent of sunflowers on a warm summer day greeted my nose.

"Ms. Whatley, a pleasure to meet you. I'm Bartholomew Morgan."

"Likewise," she said.

I sat down behind my desk and my chair squeaked in protest. Apparently, Holly either didn't care about this squeak, or purposefully left it to grate on my nerves. My vote was on the latter.

"How can I help you, Ms. Whatley?"

She returned to her seat and placed her hands on her knees. For a moment, she didn't say anything, only wrung her flower-print dress in her hands. Her lips, a shade softer than a bonfire, were pursed.

"I need you to track down my son."

A missing persons case. Not typically my forte, but it wouldn't be the first time.

"I assume the police haven't helped?"

Her eye twitched and she glanced up at me. For a moment, those light blue eyes went dark. She let go of the dress and folded her arms.

"Technically, he isn't missing."

"Well, Ms. Whatley, if he isn't missing, why do you need me?"

Maybe he owed her money, or was in a bad way with some bad people. She glanced at her lap and her cheeks flushed. Before she spoke again, she started fidgeting with her dress.

"Rudy hasn't been himself for over a year now, he's been getting sloppy at his job, and I'm afraid his actions might get a lot of people killed. I want to know what he's up to before it's too late."

"What makes you think he's dangerous, Ms. Whatley?"

I pulled out a pad of paper and started taking notes.

"He's been acting out of character for a while, getting defiant. Things were okay for a short time, but I could tell he wasn't himself. I told myself it was just the run of bad luck he was in, but I don't think that was it."

The waterworks started, so I handed her a box of tissues, which was standard issue for my line of work. You wouldn't believe the amount of crying people who end up on the other side of my desk.

"You haven't said anything that indicates he's dangerous. What did you mean?"

She went on to explain some more about his situation. I wrote down a few notes, but still wasn't sure where this was going. She was keeping something hidden, that much I knew for sure. I've seen my share of liars, cheats, and people not telling the whole truth. However, I didn't want to be rude, so I proceeded carefully.

"Go on, please," I said.

She took a deep breath, and then looked me in the eye.

"He put a lock on the door to his room, heavy duty. One day, he forgot to lock it up before he left at night, so I did what any worried mother would do. The room was a mess, which was unusual. Rudy had always been very tidy, even as a young boy. In fact, he would clean the house for me without me having to ask. I was quite grateful, as any mother would be.

"His bed was untouched, but there were blankets on the floor. He had scrawled some drawing on the walls as well, but I didn't have a chance to look much further, because he came home."

Her hands started to shake a little and her eyes stared at nothing.

"He was furious, angry that I had entered the room. He started babbling on about his work and how important it was, and that he couldn't have me interfering. Rudy had a crazy look in his eyes. I'd seen that look before."

Ms. Whatley turned away to wipe away some fresh tears. Her shoulders convulsed as she cried. I wanted to go to her, put my arm around those soft shoulders and tell her it would be okay, but I was a professional. Well... I suppose that opinion differed depending on who you talked to.

"Ms. Whatley, I can conduct surveillance on your son no problem. However, if I do find that he's involved in illegal activities, I'll have to take the proper procedures of course."

Generally the proper procedures meant calling the cops. I had been known to look the other way in certain circumstances, generally involving certain "fees;" however, never with dangerous individuals.

"Of course, I merely ask that you inform me first," she said.

I nodded. She gave me the rest of the lowdown. Apparently after the confrontation with her son, he left the house and hadn't returned. That was two days ago. I would need to see his room and she agreed to that. Before we could move further, I'd have to discuss the logistics.

"Ms. Whatley, I'm sure Holly informed you of my rates, but I want to make sure you understand that my services don't come cheap. For surveillance, I charge fifty an hour plus mileage. No more than five-hundred a day. Is that going to be an issue?"

Something told me it wouldn't.

"No, Mr. Morgan. Just please find my son and make sure he hasn't hurt anyone."

I still thought there was more to the story than she was letting on, but I could find out for myself.

"No worries, Ms. Whatley, I'll find him. I'm very good at what I do. Holly will take care of the details up front."

She rose, and I couldn't help but steal a glance at those lovely legs. We shook hands once again and I asked her a question.

"Do you have a current picture of your son, Ms. Whatley?"

"Of course."

She dug into her purse and handed me a photo. Rudy had brown hair parted down the middle. It was already starting to recede. He wore thick-rimmed glasses that pulled on his face with their weight, giving the boy a kind of tired expression. His eyes, brown in color seemed to look at nothing at all. He had a crooked smile as he held up a certificate which stated Employee of the Month in bold black letters.

"I've done a lot of research, Mr. Morgan, and I've chosen you specifically to undertake this task. Please don't disappoint me," she said.

"I'll do everything in my power to get the job done. You mentioned you had seen that look before in your son's eyes. What did you mean?"

She pulled her hand away. Not fast, but with some force.

"Actually, in my husband's eyes; burned out from duties and responsibilities, he put a bullet in his head. Rudy had the same look."

The rain was coming down even harder as I drove to Ms. Whatley's house. It was just past seven in the evening, but the skies were already dark. Pretty early for summer, but perhaps it was the overcast clouds.

I had all my equipment in the back seat. I had planned on finding Rudy as soon as I left the Whatley house; however, I needed to see his room first. More than likely there would be something in there that would put me on the trail.

The house was old, big, and located in the Avenues of Salt Lake City. It dug into the side of the hill like a parasite, unwilling to let go lest it roll down the street. Once the house was probably a glossy white, but now that color had faded and peeled with age. It looked more akin to an octogenarian marked with liver spots.

I parked the car and made my way to the front door. Several newspapers were sitting on the front porch in various states of decay along with several, colorful feathers, which reminded me of tropical birds. Perhaps Ms. Whatley owned a parrot. I double-checked the address to make sure I had the right house. The numbers matched up.

The door was larger than normal, and made from a dark-stained oak. When I knocked, the heavy thud that resonated told me it was solid. Thunder boomed in the distance, as if answering my knocks. I raised my hand to try again when the deadbolt flipped and the door opened.

The sultry form of Ms. Whatley greeted me. She had changed clothes since I last saw her at the office. Instead of a fun sun dress, she wore a pink bath robe. Her hair was damp and clung to her cheeks.

"Mr. Morgan," she said, almost a purr.

What was it about this woman? She screamed sex in such a way that it was both subtle and in my face. I had to focus on the task at hand.

"Ms. Whatley, thanks for seeing me tonight. I would like to get this matter resolved as soon as possible for you."

"I would be forever in your debt."

She opened the door wider to let me in. The house was dark, with bare light bulbs on the wall and ceiling providing a dull light. The interior of the home was somewhat Spartan, with only an old couch, and an even older coffee table with a century of water stains. It wasn't what I expected. Ms. Whatley struck me as the kind of woman that would have a house full of niceties. This seemed barely lived in.

"Just moving into the place?"

Her lips screwed into a frown, but she didn't answer. My gut was screaming for me to leave, but I wanted to see the job through. We hadn't had a decent job in a few weeks, and the money was direly needed; the rent was coming due soon.

She led me down the hall, and even with the creepy house surrounding us, I couldn't help but notice the sway of her hips. She shot me a glance from behind her shoulder and grinned. There was something predatory in her smile. Ms. Whatley was a dangerous woman; I'd have to remember that.

Rudy's room sat at the end of a long hallway which was just as empty as the greeting room. There were blank spaces on the wall where the paint was lighter marking empty homes where pictures once hanged.

His door, like the front door, was solid. A latch in the upper corner with a padlock secured the door shut. It wouldn't be too hard to open.

I reached into my pocket and pulled out my lock picking tools. Unlike in the movies, it wasn't just a magical jiggle and then, bam, presto-chango, open lock. It took more time, and a lot more precision. However, I was pretty good at it, and it didn't take long.

Rudy's room was musty, humid even as if a swamp cooler had been blowing directly into it. Yet it was hot. With the rain outside dropping the temperature, it should have been nice and cool; however, the heat was oppressive.

I walked into the room. Like the rest of the house, it was dark with a single exposed light bulb to provide light. The walls were covered with writing from different languages, some I recognized, and others I didn't. One phrase, in hastily scribbled English caught my eye—*A sacrifice for the sun, or we shall all drown in darkness, brine, and blood.*

There were printed papers depicting Mesoamerican sacrificial rituals, detailing methods, tools, and art. Dozens of depictions of people having their hearts and innards cut out, burned, and offered to old gods. There were pictures showing ancient Celtic peoples burning others alive in giant wooden structures shaped like people.

Other printouts detailed sunrise and sunset times, solar flare activity, and weather reports. I sifted through some of the papers near the bed, and found something of interest. There were over a dozen photos of the miniature island called Black Rock at the edge of the Great Salt Lake. Each photo looked like it was taken in the morning as the sun was rising. They all had dates written on the back ranging through the last few months with the most recent being a week ago. Upon further investigation, I found a pattern; the dates were weekly, exactly seven days apart. If this was the case, and Rudy kept to the pattern, he would be there tomorrow morning.

The rest of the room was filled with garbage and dirty clothes. There wasn't much else to go on.

"Do you think you can find my son, Mr. Morgan?"

"I think I have enough to go on, I'll get started right away. Please let me know if Rudy comes back."

"Of course."

I left Ms. Whatley's house with more questions than when I arrived. At least I had a direction to follow.

On the way back to the office, I put in a few calls and cashed in a few favors in an attempt to locate Rudy. If his car was spotted or he used his credit card, I'd be notified.

I called the office, but no one answered. Holly usually stayed late, so I was surprised she didn't pick up. I asked her once why she didn't go home after quitting time, which was officially six in the evening. She said it was because if no one was there to ensure everything was orderly, then the business would go to hell. Guess she didn't have much confidence in my own abilities. Who was I kidding? Without her help, I would have gone bankrupt years ago.

The next day, wanting to get a jump start on things, I pulled into the parking lot shortly after five in the morning and immediately knew something wasn't right. Rain still hammered the area, making it hard to see, but I could see enough to tell shit and a running fan had already been acquainted.

Holly's car was still parked just outside the building, the lights in the office were on, and the glass pane in the door was smashed.

Before I got out of the vehicle, I grabbed the revolver from my glove compartment. The weight told me it was still loaded. With the gun trained in front of me, I crept up to my place of business.

Glass shards cracked underneath my shoes as I walked up, reminding me of the snapping of bones for some reason. A quick glance from the outside didn't reveal anyone in the waiting area, but I couldn't be sure. I opened the door and walked in.

The office was a mess—bookshelves were overturned, Holly's chair was on its side, and the contents of her desk were strewn about. My inner office door hung by one hinge with a small flicker of light emanating from within.

I maneuvered closer to the door, placing my shoulder on the wall. Then, with a quick intake of breath I rolled around, pointing the gun toward my office. Like the waiting area, it was empty, and equally disheveled. However, sitting alone on my desk was a note.

It read: *A sacrifice for the sun, or we shall all drown in darkness, brine, and blood.*

The note must have been from Rudy, although the handwriting was different. It wasn't scribbled or chicken scratch. This handwriting spoke of confidence, measure, and meticulous care.

I rushed out the door back to the car. I knew where he would be—Black Rock.

Attempts to dial 911 on the way to Black Rock proved fruitless. Perhaps the storm was affecting the phone lines; the rain was almost a wall of water at this point. Traffic was almost non-existent with people staying inside to avoid the weather. However, the lack of traffic didn't mean much because I had to drive at a snail's pace just to stay on the road.

I passed several big rigs pulled over on the shoulder as I made my way toward Black Rock. Their blinkers served as make-shift lighthouses, keeping me oriented and away from the figurative rocky shores. I tried 911 a couple more times, and met with the same results. However, on the final try, the phone connected, but before I could say anything, static blew through the receiver. A combination of stress, weather, and the situation must have gotten to me, because I swore I heard a woman's laughter through the static; even more disturbing, I thought it was Ms. Whatley's laughter.

The rain started to dissipate as I neared Black Rock. The eastern sky grew slightly brighter as the sun started to rise, chasing away the darkness. For being seven in the morning, the sun should have been higher in the sky, painting the heavens with reds, oranges and yellows. It still looked as if it was just before dawn. Perhaps it was the clouds, perhaps something else.

A car fitting the description of Rudy's beat up vehicle was pulled over underneath an overpass. With the rain slowing down to a mere trickle, the stubby column of earth that was Black Rock jutted out of the shore of the Great Salt Lake. It stood alone, a miniature mesa next to a dead lake. A flash of movement near the base of the rock caught my attention. Two figures moved around the rock and out of sight: Rudy and Holly.

I parked the car, grabbed my pistol, and made my way toward the iconic rock island. The air was warm, warmer than it should have been. The rain made everything humid, creating a sticky sheen across my face. I hopped the railing along the road, and trudged through brush. It only took a few steps to soak my pants and shoes.

Everyone had differing opinions on what the Great Salt Lake smelled like. To me, it was a dead smell, almost sulphurous. Some days, when the winds were right, I could even smell it in my office. Today, standing in the heat and steam of the morning it was no less potent.

As I neared the rocky tower, everything went silent. The rain stopped completely, the wind died down to nothing, and only my ragged breath made any noise at all. Well, that and the squish-squish of my footsteps through the muddy shore.

I stopped to regulate my breathing, and the muffled sound of a woman's cry caught my ear. It was Holly, I knew it deep down. I rushed to the other side of the Black Rock with my gun at the ready. What awaited me almost broke my sanity.

Rudy was there, with Holly tied and gagged next to him. He looked different from the picture Ms. Whatley had given me. Rudy was gaunt, bone-thin, with a scraggly beard covering his face. His eyes and face were red, irritated, and angry. It seemed Holly hit him with an ample shot of WD-40. That was my Holly.

My presence didn't seem to faze him. He turned and began lighting candles. He had a large knife made from something that looked like obsidian. The way the blade seemed to radiate darkness made me think it was much more than mere obsidian. That, in itself, wasn't what made me stop and question my place on this earth, it was what was in the rocks above Rudy.

From what I could gather, it was Ms. Whatley. Her dark hair rained down on pale, naked shoulders, revealing the tattoo that was only hinted at during our previous meeting. The tattoo was a spiral of strange symbols and letters that didn't make any sense to me, but hurt my eyes if I looked at them too hard. She was entirely naked, covered only by her wild hair, but where her legs should have been was instead a serpentine tail covered in colorful feathers. She scrambled up the rocks, gliding across the vertical surface as if it were mere steps, climbing with long, clawed hands. Then, she cast her gaze toward me and smiled.

Her eyes glowed a brilliant blue and I almost lost myself in her hypnotic stare. She was beautiful, savage, and dangerous as ever.

If Rudy noticed her, he didn't give any indication. The boy lit the last candle then grabbed Holly. She gave another cry, kicked out, and toppled Rudy. Holly tried to scramble away, but Rudy was quick to recover and grabbed her by the hair and pulled her to the ground. He straddled her prone form, bringing the obsidian blade to her neck.

"I'm sorry, I don't want to, but it needs to happen," he said.

His words broke my trance, and grabbed my attention. I glanced back to Ms. Whatley, but she was gone.

"Let her go," I said, aiming the gun at him.

He looked up with ragged eyes sunk deep into his skull. It was still dark out, but I could tell he hadn't shaved in over a week. Tears streamed down his face.

"I... I can't," he said.

"Sure you can. Let her go and we can get you some help."

He started to sob then, his shoulders shuddering with each cry. Rudy muttered something, but I couldn't quite make it out as he wiped his face with his free hand. Holly tried to roll away, but he pushed her head back into the sand.

"Don't hurt her, Rudy. Let's sort this out, get you back to your mother, and call it a day. How's that sound?"

"She's not my mother," he said.

"Come again?"

He looked up, boring through me with his dead eyes. I'd seen my share of crazy folk, but Rudy took the cake.

"Do you think I want to do this? Do you think I enjoy killing people? I detest it, but I was chosen. Chosen just like you," he said, pointing a finger at me.

He was talking crazy, but talking meant not killing. So I egged him on.

"What do you mean, chosen?"

Rudy still held on to Holly with one hand by the hair. With his other hand, he rubbed his forehead and muttered something unintelligible again. That was the hand with the knife, the dangerous hand. I took a few steps closer when he wasn't looking. If things went south, I wanted to be as close as possible.

The sunrise should have been above the Wasatch Mountains by now, painting the valley sky in brilliant hues. However, it was still dark, with only a slight hint of sun way behind the clock. I didn't have much time to think about it given the current circumstances.

"Only the chosen can make the sacrifices. I don't know why. Brine and blood, brine and blood."

Rudy looked past me and his eyes grew wide. He started to tremble and almost lost his grip on Holly. She fought with a renewed fervor as she glanced behind me.

The water behind me started to churn, and cold, salty spray hit my back. Not wanting to divert my attention from Rudy, I gave a cursory glance behind to see what was happening. The salty water was boiling and whipping up into a froth. Before I turned my gaze back to Rudy, something rolled above the surface of the water. I couldn't tell what it was exactly, but it was black, covered in a slick slime, and ropey.

"What's going on?" I asked, to no one in particular.

The scent of sunflowers crept to my nose, and I felt a presence behind me.

"*A sacrifice for the sun, or we shall all drown in darkness, brine, and blood.*"

It was Ms. Whatley's voice, or the thing that was Ms. Whatley. Still sexy and sultry, her voice made me think inappropriate things despite the events that were unfolding.

"*The sacrifice must be made, or the darkness shall drown everything*," she said.

"No more! I can't, no more," Rudy said, slapping his forehead hard several times causing blood to well up and roll down his face.

"Rudy, just let her go. No one has to be sacrificed here," I said, taking a couple steps closer.

He looked up at me, then past me to the Great Salt Lake. Tears mixed with the blood and rolled down his cheeks. The sky grew dark and only the dim glow of the candles gave off any light. Something large rose from the waters behind me. I wanted to look, but something deep down in my guts told me not to, that if I turned around, it would be the end.

Rudy looked to Holly, and wiped his face.

"I'm sorry," he said.

Rudy raised the knife high. Holly screamed and I squeezed the trigger of my revolver. There was a blinding flash as the gun went off in my hand. The bullet struck Rudy square in the chest and arterial blood painted the rocks around him, dousing the candles.

The wind kicked up, roaring around us. I couldn't hear Holly's screams anymore, only the wind. With the candles out, I was cast in pitch dark. I fell to my knees and covered my face as bits of sand and rock whipped all about me.

Then, I heard her voice. It held a relieved tone. I no longer found it sexy.

"You are chosen. I knew you wouldn't disappoint me. A sacrifice for the sun, or we shall all drown in darkness, brine, and blood."

With those words the wind stopped and sunlight appeared from behind the mountains. I turned toward the lake, happy to see nothing but calm waters along its surface. Where ever that thing, that leviathan had come from, it had returned. I crawled over to Holly and held her in my arms. She wasn't crying anymore, but held her knees and rocked back and forth. She wouldn't look me in the eye, but kept a watchful gaze out to the water.

Rudy lay in the sand on his back, bent at the knees. He had a smile on his face. The obsidian dagger was gone.

I don't know what happened that morning, if it was real or not. I couldn't find Ms. Whatley after the incident. It was as if she never existed. Her house on the hill was just as I left it. After some digging, I found out that she never owned the house, nor did Rudy. I suppose they were squatting or something. Came to find out Rudy's parents died a long time ago in a car accident and he wasn't even related to anyone closely resembling a Ms. Whatley.

Holly stayed on board with me, despite the incident. I think she found strength staying close to someone who had been there. We don't talk about it much, but I can only surmise what she saw in those waters. She doesn't go near the Great Salt Lake, and insists on being home before dark. Holly's still as strong as ever, giving me shit when I need it, hell, even sometimes when I don't, but a part of her died out there at Black Rock.

What I do know is it isn't over. It's been almost a year, and the days are getting shorter, darker earlier than normal. A few days ago a package arrived at the office. There were no post marks or a return address. It was a flat, rectangular box wrapped in plain brown paper. Inside were Rudy's obsidian dagger, a colorful feather that smelled of sunflowers and a note.

A sacrifice for the sun, or we shall all drown in darkness, brine, and blood.

About the story: "Brine & Blood" appeared in the anthology, *It Came from the Great Salt Lake*, published by Griffin Publishers in February of 2016. It was an anthology put together by the Utah Chapter of the Horror Writers Association (Note: there was no sponsorship or endorsement by the HWA on the anthology, the Chapter merely helped put it together). At the time I'd been listening to a lot of urban fantasy short stories that dealt with detectives or cops in fantastic settings. I wanted to try my hand at one, and thus, "Brine & Blood" was conceived. I had a lot of fun with the character, and I wouldn't be surprised if we meet Bart again at some point. I mean, come on... a sacrifice must be made again, right?

"The Deep Well"

The sun descended behind the steep jungle mountains, allowing the shadows to crawl from the dark places of the earth. The gloom made things difficult. Things like fighting and killing.

"Come on, more are coming."

Sebastian's was no more than a whisper, yet to his ears, it was louder than church bells on the Sabbath. The jungle responded, waiting with bated breath as silence blanketed the pair of conquistadors.

Guillermo nodded while scratching a bushy beard the color of mud. He planted a boot and yanked his sword from the prone body of one of the natives.

The dead man on the ground was one of the scouts. Unlike the older warriors of the tribe, the scout wore only a loin cloth and a necklace of decorative bone. The ones that followed close behind would be better equipped.

"This way," Sebastian said.

There was the snap of a branch just beyond some thick brush. Sebastian hesitated for half a breath then darted into the jungle. Guillermo followed not a second behind. Sebastian grabbed the big man and pulled him prone. The jungle ate the pair, hiding them from view.

A dozen warriors ran past, decorated with animal hide chest pieces, armed with spears and large wooden swords lined with shards of obsidian. Sebastian had seen one of the warriors take the head off another man with one swing during a particularly vicious battle. Sebastian knew when he left Spain to come to this new world it would be dangerous. They all accepted that risk when they stepped on the boat. Yet, he wasn't ready for the things in the darkness. The strange noises in the deep caves or the way the tribal shamans looked at him from afar: a dead look, as if something peered from behind their eyes.

The new tribe they found on their second trip acted differently than the other natives in the region. They stayed away from the small tribe as much as possible, and there were rumors of horrible rituals to ancient and darker things.

He regretted leaving Spain the moment they set sail, but he didn't have a choice. Sebastian needed to accomplish this conquest. His victory in the new world would carry over to the old, lifting his family from poverty into a better life. They depended on him to do all he could here and return safely.

Sebastian and Guillermo waited until the warriors were gone before creeping back onto the foot path. Guillermo brushed leaves and dirt from his armor while Sebastian skulked up the trail to scout ahead. The warriors were nowhere to be seen. Perhaps he'd make it home after all.

"Hermano," Guillermo said, his words slurred.

The big man swayed, and leaned against a tree. He took two steps before falling to the dirt. Sebastian ran to his brother's side just as something hit him in the neck. He slapped a hand up and pulled a feathered dart out of his skin. His vision blurred and then weightlessness took over. Everything went black.

Sebastian dreamt of a city under the water which stretched further than his imagination could comprehend. Larger than any of the cities he'd seen in Spain; the place in his dream was built entirely of gold. As he wandered the golden streets the weight of a thousand eyes peered at him from behind locked doors and blackened windows. Strange symbols decorated the walls depicting all manner of debauchery.

The architecture was somewhat familiar to that of the temples and cities of the natives, yet there was something different, something older to it. As if the temples beneath the water were a distant memory to those above ground.

Soon, he found himself in front of a tall building of coral, gilded in the precious metal he'd come to find. The underwater tower rose far above him, further than he could see. A set of stairs climbed up the tower in a spiral, leading to a dais built on the side of the wall. A figure sat in a large throne overseeing everything below. It was hard to make out any details, but the figure's eyes glowed with a bright blue energy. At the figure's side, leaning against the throne, was a mighty axe made of crystal, glowing with the same azure power.

A pulse emanated from the tower—something breathing, something large. Voices rose in the distance, thousands of them all chanting a single word over and over. Sebastian couldn't make out the language, though it sounded similar to the tongue of the native tribes.

The chanting grew in intensity, becoming louder and louder as the doors of the tower opened. The glowing light became brighter, pouring forth from an open hole in the ground from within the temple. An intense feeling of hunger gripped at Sebastian's insides, overtaking all other senses and thoughts. The chants soared into a crescendo and awful sigils on the floor flared to life.

The dream and the sense of weightlessness vanished when Sebastian crashed into a pile of bodies. The air blasted from his lungs while the coppery taste of blood filled his mouth. He rolled off the corpses onto the dirt. Several forms stood at the top of the pit staring back down at him, shadowy silhouettes with the sun setting at their backs. They chanted the same word from his dream, a name: Chaactulu.

Sebastian got to his feet and tried to walk, but the motion caused a wave of nausea to break upon his body. He dropped to his knees, emptying his stomach. The ground called to him and without thinking, he rested his head against the dirt. It was wet and smelled of decay, but it didn't matter. He needed to rest his eyes.

"Wake up. We need to move."

The voice was gravel, oiled with phlegm.

"Guillermo?"

"Yes. Come on, we need to find a way out of this hell-hole."

Sebastian propped himself up with his elbows. Guillermo grabbed Sebastian's arm, the man's hand gripping him like a crab's claw. With one quick heave he lifted Sebastian to his feet.

Sebastian steadied himself and took in his surroundings. It was as if the cavern waited for him to regain his senses before hitting him in the face with the stench. It was the kind of smell that saturated clothes and stuck to the inside of a person's lungs. It was a stench that haunted dreams.

A pile of bodies lay broken near the pit's wall: friends, comrades in arms, and others from the ship. They hadn't survived the fall. Perhaps they even softened the blow for his own landing. There were other bodies as well, bodies of the natives. However, unlike the Spanish warriors, the natives bore signs of ritual sacrifice. Some were decapitated, while others were missing their hearts.

Sebastian knelt next to one of his fallen comrades. The man's face was a bloody mess, puffed up and swollen in death. He had known him well, having made the first trip to the new world with him.

"Vaya con dios," Sebastian whispered.

Before he stood, something caught his eye. The man's arm was missing from the elbow down. He took a closer look and found that it appeared something had chewed it off. Sebastian looked to the other bodies and found similar wounds. Many were missing hands, feet, or even portion of their faces. Something had come up here to feed.

Sebastian let his hand fall to the hilt of his sword.

"Why did they leave our equipment untouched?" Sebastian asked.

"No idea. Let's just count it as a blessing."

"Think we can climb it?" He asked, pointing to the rock wall.

"No way, hermano, that rock's slicker than a port whore. Perhaps with some rope and help from above."

His brother let the obvious go unspoken, but the thought bored through Sebastian's brain: they would have to go through the caves. The cavern funneled into a tunnel leading downward. Water trickled from an opening in the rock wall and followed the passageway. It created a bubbling which echoed down into the dark. Guillermo pulled a torch from his pack and sparked it to life with his flint and steel.

They gathered what equipment they could from their fallen comrades, said a prayer, and then started toward the tunnel. The sun peeked one last time over the pit as they descended into the earth. A last ray of the day's light followed them as far as it could before darkness chased it away. The cluster of stars had reformed into a straight line, shining brighter than any other star in the sky. Sebastian spat and cursed to no one in particular before following Guillermo.

Within a dozen steps they came across a large wooden pole buried in the ground. Frayed cordage hung off it like discarded seaweed and littered the surroundings in various states of decay. There was a pile of rags lay near the pole and Sebastian used the tip of his boot to rummage through the rags.

"Look at this," he said.

Guillermo moved closer bringing the torch's light with him. "What is it?"

"Don't these look like the clothes the natives dress their women in?"

Guillermo stared at the clothes for a moment before grunting something unintelligible.

"Doesn't matter, let's keep moving. We don't have many torches," the big man said.

Sebastian nodded and followed him, but something gnawed at his thoughts. The word and whispers from his dream. He could almost hear it in the echoes of the running water—almost.

They walked for hours, always downward. Sometimes the grade was so gradual only the constant stream of water was the only signal they still headed lower into the earth. Other times, they came to drop-offs that required them to climb.

Guillermo struck another torch.

"One more after this, hermano.

"God willing, it will lead us out."

As they continued their trek, something glittered and winked from the stream bed. Sebastian leaned down and rubbed a finger across the rocks. He brought his hand close to face. Then, eyes wide, he grabbed Guillermo by the shirt and pulled him close.

"Look! Look at this!"

"Is that?" Guillermo asked.

"Yes! Gold!"

The fine powder caught the light of the torch and sparkled under its flame. They ran their fingers across the walls and floors. Gold dust covered everything. Sebastian knelt and picked up a nugget the size of his hand.

"My god, look at this!" Guillermo let out a loud guffaw. The big man stuffed gold nuggets into his belt pouch until he couldn't cinch it closed. "We're rich!"

"Not if we can't get out of here," Sebastian said. The mirth shattered on the rocks of reality. This discovery could pull his family from the dregs and into a life of luxury. He just needed to get out and come back with more men. They would claim the tunnel for the Kingdom of Spain. The strange tribe of savages wouldn't be able to withstand an organized contingent of soldiers. The reward for such a find would be grand. They just needed to get out, which at this point was simple in concept, difficult in execution.

The tunnel opened to a large cavern. The flickering of the torch did little to fight the dark for it was a gloom not used to the audacity and ignorance of the light. As they stepped across the threshold and into the cavern, Sebastian couldn't fight the feeling he had been here before. Their footsteps echoed through the gloom disappearing into infinity.

Something scraped along the ground to their right breaking the spell of silence. Sebastian stopped and drew his sword. Guillermo thrust the torch out in front of him. The firelight danced with the darkness. A couple rocks rolled across the ground in front of them. Yet, try as they might, they couldn't see what had moved through the shadow.

"Be on your guard," Sebastian said.

The trickle of water grew louder as they continued their journey. As they moved forward, more and more streams appeared on either side of them and ran parallel, only to converge into a larger rush of water. They found even more tributaries as they moved further into the cavern. It wasn't much longer before they came to the outskirts of a city that took their breath away.

Large buildings made of gold and rock spiraled far into the darkness, finally eaten by the shadow to be unseen. Sebastian stopped and almost dropped his sword.

The buildings from his dream stood before him.

"Oh Lord and Savior, save us," Sebastian whispered.

Sebastian shook his head and took a step backward. He grabbed Guillermo by the shoulder stopping him from moving any closer to the time-forgotten buildings.

"We need to leave."

Guillermo looked from the strange buildings back to Sebastian. He swept his arm out wide toward the darkness.

"Where are we going to go, hermano? Where?"

"I've seen this place before, in a dream."

"We've all dreamt of this place. El Dorado! The city of gold!"

"You fool! That place is a myth."

The sense of being watched by something in the darkness increased and Sebastian gripped his sword tighter. He tried to find comfort in the cold hard steel, but it did little to calm his nerves. The sputter of the torch didn't help in the slightest.

"Damn! We need to find more light. I don't want to be trapped down here unable to see," Guillermo said.

As if on cue, the torch died and the darkness swallowed them as a whale would devour a school of fish.

"Don't move," Guillermo hissed.

The sounds of Guillermo rummaging through his pack filled Sebastian's ears, as well as another sound.

A scraping, wet noise.

"What's that?" Sebastian asked.

Something brushed his shoulder. Sebastian dipped low and reached out with an open hand. The stench of fish overpowered the damp cavern, filling his senses. The distinct strike of steel on flint cracked out and sparks rent the dark around them. The explosion of light left ghost images dancing behind his eyes. Then, in a whoosh, the last torch lit and pushed the blackness away. There wasn't anyone there but Guillermo.

Sebastian swept his hand across his shoulder. It was covered in a light sheen of transparent slime. He moved closer to the torch to get a better look.

"Look," Guillermo said.

A strange set of wet tracks led toward a building. They were bigger than a man's footprints, and sported three large toes.

"What kind of devilry is this?" Sebastian asked. "Come on, I need your light!" Perhaps they could force the newcomer to reveal the exit.

They ran to the building. Sebastian held his sword out in front of him and shouldered up next to the door. Guillermo saddled up to the other side. The big man brought the torch forward letting the dim light flicker into the building.

Shapes moved just beyond the threshold.

A croak from the shadows brought them both to their guard. Sebastian raised his sword and dropped into a fighting stance. Guillermo followed suit and held his weapon high above his head, ready to strike at whatever lurked beyond the torch's light. The croak bellowed again, this time answered by another. Then another.

"Ready yourself," Sebastian said. He tried to remember everything he learned from his martial training. Anything at all that would save him and take him back to his family. They depended on him. However, nothing prepared him for what was to come.

A blur of pallid color rushed from the shadows and drove Guillermo to the ground. The torch fell from the man's grasp and rolled away. The light jumped and danced as the torch skipped across the rocks. It was hard to see, but Sebastian lunged forward and slashed with his sword. The blade bit deep into the thing's back and ripped a wail of pure hate from its lungs. The creature continued to thrash until Sebastian planted a boot against its head. It rolled off Guillermo and shuddered. Sebastian drove his sword down in a powerful chop that bit into the creature's side.

"What in the name of God?" Guillermo asked between deep breaths. Blood streamed down the man's face in tiny rivulets, but he directed his attention toward the thing on the ground.

Sebastian retrieved the torch and pushed it close to the creature. He wished he hadn't.

It was taller than a man, and lanky. Its skin was the pallor of seaweed, and not unlike the catfish Sebastian used to catch in the channels near his home. A thin web connected all of its clawed fingers. Two, bulging eyes glazed with death adorned its face.

Guillermo thrust his sword into the creature's head and twisted. It flopped around for a moment, and then flopped no more.

"Go back to hell, demon."

A croak bleated from further in the darkness. More cries trumpeted in response and then moved closer.

"Come on," Sebastian said, handing the torch back to Guillermo.

They ran down the golden streets of the ancient city. The torch sputtered on its last breath as they continued. Sebastian gripped his sword tighter but it did little to fight the suffocating dark. The croaking of the creatures came closer and closer.

"What do we do?" Guillermo asked.

"We-"

Grimy hands with webbed fingers grabbed Guillermo, pulling him through a window-like opening on the side of a building. The big man struggled, dropping his torch and trying his best to pry the hands off him, but they were too strong. Sebastian moved in to help, but more hands grabbed Guillermo and pulled him into the darkness. Guillermo screamed and cursed, before he was suddenly silenced.

"Guillermo!"

There was no answer. The torch died, casting everything into complete darkness.

"Guillermo?'

In response there was the sound of shuffling feet in the darkness, moving closer and closer. Sebastian, unable to see anything used his hand to guide himself along the wall as quickly as possible. IIc did his best to put some distance between him and his attackers, but the going was agonizingly slow.

A pale blue glow appeared in the gloom. The light was faint, but it lit up like a beacon in the pitch black of the cave. The cerulean glow silhouetted the building in front of him. Sebastian moved with a renewed purpose.

He could almost hear his wife's laughter as he ran through the streets of the long forgotten city. She danced in the corner of his eye, twirled to music only she could hear. A smile gripped his face and he almost laughed. That laughter died in his throat when he rounded the corner.

Before him lay the tower from his dream. The blue glow emanated from a series of strange sigils on the floor. Sebastian stopped and took an involuntary step back.

"We were fools to ever come here," Sebastian said.

The fish-men blocked the streets, surrounding him. They swayed from side to side in a horrible rhythm while looking up into the dark above the tower.

The sigils flared brighter and then dimmed as if drawing in breath.

A dank gust blew over him, a wind that carried the ancient stink of meat and stagnant water. Sebastian threw an arm over his face to block the light and the smell. Water splashed somewhere so violently it reminded of him of a shark jumping from the ocean's depths.

Despair hit him, stealing the hope from his guts. It almost took all of his confidence, but a single grain remained. His inner grit turned that grain into a pearl. Sebastian would get home to his family.

He turned his back to the tower and rushed the wall of creatures. If they noticed his onslaught, they didn't let on. Sebastian put the tip of his sword through the first one's throat. A brackish liquid spewed forth and the thing dropped to the gilded street.

Sebastian drove the pommel of his weapon into the temple of another and it fell with a sick crack. Two more creatures stepped up to fill the gaps of their fallen comrades and joined in the dance. Sebastian let out a growl cutting one of the newcomers down only to find another take its place.

The sigils lit up again, brighter than before, followed by another blast of foul air. Something carried on the gust this time—words. Sebastian didn't understand them at first, but little by little his brain constructed something to make sense of the utterance. He'd never heard the words before, but deep down on some level, his body knew what they meant—something was coming.

The creatures croaked the words in unison, over and over. Sebastian turned and faced the tower once again. Something hid in the darkness behind the pale glow of the sigils: something large.

The wall of creatures parted, making an opening for *it* to come through. It was taller than the rest, towering over them like a fabled giant. Its skin was grey and mottled with scales, and it was adorned in a mismatch of rotting skins, both animal and human. It gripped a giant axe made of crystal in one webbed hand, and its large taloned feet clacked against the stone floor as it walked. It wore a helmet made from the skull of some creature, foreign to Sebastian, but looking similar to a giant python. Underneath the helmet, a fishlike face smiled at him, revealing rows of sharp, glasslike teeth.

It came to a stop in front of him, taking heavy breathes. Then, it spoke. Its voice was harsh and guttural, and Sebastian couldn't understand any of it, except one word: Chaactulu. The word sent voices whispering in his ear, gibbering mad things that he couldn't understand. His vision blurred, and for a half a moment, there was something else in the cavern with them—something old and ancient. Something that was hungry.

Sebastian had faced hunger and starvation before. Months at sea and time fighting wars had forged his stomach. However, this hunger was much more than that. The feeling that ripped through him was primal and dominated everything. He wanted to consume the entire world.

As fast as the feeling came, it disappeared. Yet, unlike the feeling, the enormous creature still stood before him. It raised the crystal axe, and pointed it towards Sebastian. The blade glowed blue, the same color as the sigils, providing even more light.

Seeing no other option, Sebastian stood straight and brought his sword up into a salute, then crouched into a fighting stance. The fish people cheered, yelling in their language and filling the cavern with a cacophony of sound. His opponent smiled, spit something on the floor and charged forward.

It swung the axe at his head with a speed Sebastian hadn't seen before. He dropped to one knee and rolled away as the weapon cut the air where he had been moments before. As he rolled to his feet, he had to turn to dodge the return blow that would have cleaved him in half.

Sebastian spun and drove his sword forward with a deadly thrust. The creature parried it with the axe. His blade vibrated violently when it met the crystal and he almost dropped his weapon.

The creature grabbed him by the shirt with his free hand and pulled him in close, then drove its head down, smashing Sebastian's face and nose.

Pain lanced through his skull and the familiar taste of blood filled his mouth. His vision blurred for a moment as his eyes filled with tears. The creature reared its head back for another blow, but Sebastian drove the pommel of his sword into the creature's temple.

The weapon hit the bone helmet, skewing it to one side and sending a splinter of it flying off into the crowd. The creature let him go and Sebastian staggered to the side wiping the blood and tears from his face.

After a moment of messing with the helmet, the creature growled and flung it from its head. It hit the ground with a loud clack and rolled away. Sebastian fell into his fighting stance once again. His opponent was stronger and faster, but this wasn't the first time Sebastian had fought someone with those qualities. He had to be smarter.

He raised his sword, striking at the creature's head and met resistance when it brought the axe up to block. Sebastian struck again, once at the head, then again on the other side of the creature's face. Both blocked again. He took a step back, then another, waiting for the right moment. The creature rushed in, and as it started to raise its weapon for a strike, Sebastian hopped forward and swung his sword once again at the creature's head.

This time, as it moved to block, Sebastian dropped his hips and shoulder bringing the sword down for a low attack instead of a high attack. His sword bit into the creature's thigh, slicing through scales and flesh before hitting bone. Putrid blood the color of dirty seawater spilled forth, coating the rocky ground in a slick slime.

The creature howled and dropped to its knee. Sebastian, wanting to take advantage of the situation, swung his sword at the creature's neck for the killing blow. The creature caught the blade with its webbed hand, taking two of its fingers off before becoming lodged in bone.

It roared and grabbed Sebastian by the leg, flinging him to the ground. His head smacked a rock and his ears started to ring. He tried to clear his vision, but everything was spinning. The last thing he saw was a swarm of fish men rushing toward him.

Sebastian woke to a sound he thought he would never hear again, the sound of Guillermo singing. The big man sang a song from his home village, it was a quiet tune about a fox outwitting some hunters. For a moment, Sebastian thought he was back on the ship. It would account for why his clothes were wet.

He opened his eyes and found himself chained to the wall by his foot. His muscles protested any movement, and he was certain one of his ribs was broken, making each breath laborious. Guillermo was in a similar situation, chained to the wall. The big man's eye was swollen shut, and he had a nasty gash on his forehead that was dripping blood into his beard.

On the opposite wall, several women were chained. They were nude, disheveled and avoided his gaze. They were a mix of native women from various tribes, but there was one thing each had in common. They were all with child.

"Where are we?" Sebastian asked.

"Hell, hermano."

They were inside a building with the walls stretching further than he could see. A massive hole in the floor was surrounded by the strange sigils, all of which were pulsing with a blue light. Water bubbled up from the hole, which was slowly filling the room. The sigils' glow, covered with water, created chaotic, dancing patterns all across the walls.

A fish man dragged the body of one of his fellow conquistadors over to the well, and pushed it over the hole. It floated there for a moment before *something* dragged it beneath the water.

One of the women started to moan and grabbed her belly. Sebastian stared in horror as something moved inside her. He'd seen babies moving from within before, but this was something else. It was long and sinuous. Several more moved within the woman's belly and she coughed up blood before leaning her head back.

The water covering the hole stirred as bubbles rose from the depths. The sigils flared bright, almost blinding, and the fish-men started to chant the word, Chaactulu over and over.

The water began to rise even faster, and soon it came up to his chest.

"Do you hear it, hermano?"

He was about to ask what, but then he did hear it. The whispers of thousands speaking to him in a language that few mortals have ever heard. This time he understood what they were saying. It was that moment he knew he would never see his family again.

The water continued to rise, inching its way to his face. One of the women let out a long cry before there was the sound of something tearing, followed by a splash. The water churned over by the women, reminding him of the time when he saw a school of sharks feeding on a seal carcass.

He lifted his head as high as he could, looking up to save his final breaths. There was something far above that he hadn't caught before, an opening giving him a view of the night sky. As he watched and waited for the water to overtake him, he caught three dots of light above, slowly moving into position. The stars were aligning.

The water rose over his face and he turned his attention back to the hole, wishing instantly that he hadn't.

Sebastian's vision started to fade as his body was deprived of air; however, he caught a glimpse of *it*. A giant clawed hand, bigger than some ships he had seen, came forth from the hole and clutched the edge. Thousands of tentacles started to float up, swaying in the currents like seaweed. Chaactulu had arrived.

About the story: "The Deep Well" was one of my first forays into pulp fiction. I wanted to write something akin to the Conan stories penned by Robert E. Howard, but with a

Lovecraftian twist. This story went through a lot of iterations before it found itself a home with *Broadswords and Blasters Issue 2* in July of 2017.

For one, and let this be a lesson to you, I was called out by the editors who were both expert historians that my story was crossing cultures, (I was using Mayan sacrificial practices to an Aztec deity), big old WAMP-WAMP, there, right? Well, luckily for me, they said I could feel free to submit again in the future, even this very piece if it underwent significant revisions. The challenge was accepted. I went to work rewriting the story, sent it in, and we had a winner. It really goes to show that tons of research needs to happen if you plan on writing anything historical.

"All Aboard"

Hyrum, we're going to be brothers forever right? Aren't we?

Hyrum Woolley's eyes popped open and he tried to scream; however, he couldn't find the breath necessary to create the sound. He sat up in bed and grabbed at his throat as if the action would free whatever force had hold of him. Hyrum rolled out of bed and crashed onto the floor of his dingy bedroom. A pale blue glow from a cheap night-light bathed the room offering a meager look at things, things that started to blur as his vision narrowed.

Finally, his lungs kicked into action and whatever previously blocked his airway, let loose allowing sweet oxygen to enter his system. All at once his vision snapped back into focus as he took in big gasps of air. Tears ran down his face and he shuffled into the corner next to his bed and sobbed, holding his knees close to his chest while rocking back and forth.

As it happened every time before, it took him almost ten minutes to regain his composure. Hyrum flipped on the lights and walked to a calendar which was the only thing decorating his walls other than dust and a cheaply framed certificate of graduation from the Bridgerland Applied Technology Center of Law Enforcement.

He grabbed a red marker hanging on a string and found the appropriate date before drawing a large X in the box. Several other X's decorated the page, yet this week had an X marked every day. The fits always were worse near the anniversary of his brother's death.

It was only a little past four in the morning. He didn't have to check in with dispatch for another two hours, but sleep wasn't an option anymore. Unless he took a heavy dose of medication, he wouldn't be able to sleep again today, not after a fit like that.

Hyrum grabbed a pair of pants off the floor and hiked them on. He sucked in his gut, forced the button to clasp, and relaxed. The waistband strained under the force and dug into his belly. He needed to get a new pair of pants today.

A year ago, the thought would have been more along the lines of, he needed to lose some weight. But he eventually gave up on all that bullshit and just accepted his body. He fished around the room until he found a belt. Two makeshift holes already adorned the aged leather, and he almost had to make a new one when he cinched it on. He sat back on the bed out of breath.

Thunder boomed outside and shook the windowpanes of the small house. He stopped brushing his teeth mid-stroke and peeked out through the blinds of his bathroom window. Rain poured from dark twisted clouds rolling and dancing through the night sky like fighting cats. Thunder raged again and its roar rattled deep in his bones.

Hyrum finished getting ready for work by pulling a broken comb through his receding blonde hair. He put on an off-white button-up shirt along with a maroon tie. To finish it off, he grabbed his badge and service weapon and clipped them to his belt; the weight of which applied even more strain to the cracked leather barely holding onto his pants. He applied two quick spurts of Old Spice before walking to the living room to grab his coat. By the time he stepped outside and onto his porch, the storm raged in the distance. Instead of the freshly washed smell and clean feeling that usually came with the rain, the air was sticky and left a film on his skin.

He opened the door to his Ford Crown Victoria Police Interceptor and fired the engine to life. The windshield wipers swept lazily across the window, leaving streaks of grime in his view. Hyrum turned the radio on and keyed the mic.

"Dispatch, this is Woolley, I'm 10-41."

"Morning Hyrum," replied a high-pitched feminine voice.

"Morning, Lacey."

Hyrum drove from his home which sat on the outskirts of Elk Hollow, Utah. Elk Hollow was a small farming community situated between the middle of nowhere and the edge of the world. Within ten minutes he was at the town's one and only gas station and mini-store, *Raven's Fuel & Sundry.* He walked in through the door and an electronic beep warbled to life from a small set of speakers.

"Marlene, I'll never get used to that," Hyrum said.

"Morning, Hyrum. Listen to it all day and it becomes background noise. You here for your usual?"

"Yes ma'am," Hyrum replied.

Marlene was a short, squat woman, with long gray hair that reached her knees. She wore a simple black apron with a cross-stitched Raven on the front along with thick, horn-rimmed glasses that made her look more like an owl. Her hands shook slightly, and she had a slight hump in her back, but she still showed up to work at the gas station every morning at five without fail.

"Well I'm sorry, but we didn't get our delivery this morning, I'm afraid we're out of those sweet Danishes you love," she said.

"You've got to be kidding me. You've never run out of that stuff before," Hyrum said.

Marlene shuffled close to Hyrum and touched him on the shoulder. She grabbed his elbow with her arthritic hands and led him to the coffee pot.

"I know, the delivery boy, Terrell, he's always been punctual, and never missed a delivery for the last three years. Strange of him not to call or anything," she said.

Hyrum looked at the coffee pot and scanned the pastries in the display that sat next to it; old donuts, a muffin, and two bananas. In other words, nothing that caught his eye or his appetite. He let out a sigh and filled his travel mug with coffee, and grabbed a Snickers bar from the candy rack.

"What did you think of that storm?" Marlene asked.

"Kind of crazy, never seen clouds like that before," Hyrum replied.

"I drove to work through that chaos, I saw the wind blew down the old Tillerman barn," she said as she scanned the candy bar through the register.

Hyrum's radio blared to life on his belt.

"Hey, Hyrum," Lacey's voice said through the receiver.

"Yeah, go ahead," Hyrum replied.

"I think you should come on down to the station, we may have a situation here." The sound of a crying woman in the background came through the speaker.

"What's going on?" Hyrum asked.

"We have a missing person case," Lacey replied.

"10-4, I'm on my way."

Hyrum paid for the coffee and candy, then turned to head out of the shop.

"It's that storm Hyrum, nothing good can come from a storm like that. Just you wait and see."

Carol Grains sobbed uncontrollably in the lobby of the small dispatch center that doubled as Elk Hollow's police station. She sat on an uncomfortable wooden bench in front of the welcome desk with a mound of used and crumpled tissues piled next to her. Deputy Charles Jensen sat nearby with one hand on her shoulder and the other holding a small notepad. Lacey stood close to the phones, but as far away as the cord on her headsets would allow, her arms folded across her chest. She wore a look of concern but brightened visibly when Hyrum walked in.

"What's going on?" Hyrum asked.

Everyone looked up and Carol stood, spilling the snowy tissues across the floor. Deputy Jensen opened his mouth to say something but Carol beat him to it.

"My son's missing, Sheriff! You need to find him. He went out last night and..." she said in one quick breath as if the words had waited on the tip of her tongue and leaped at the chance for freedom.

Hyrum held up his hand and walked close to her. As he neared, he walked through a cloud of heavy perfume that smelled of lilacs and jasmine. He let out a cough to clear his throat but the sweet stench fought its way in, eliciting a spasm of hacks and sputters to rip from his lungs.

"Okay, first of all, when was the last time you saw him? Robert, right?" Hyrum asked, opening a notepad of his own.

"Yes, Robert Ashley Grains, he's 17, and I saw him last night around six," Carol said, grabbing another tissue from her massive leather purse. "He left on a date with his girlfriend. I told him to be home by midnight, but I didn't wait up. He always came home on time before, but this time, his car wasn't in the driveway."

Hyrum made some notes on the pad. Deputy Jensen stood and walked back toward Lacey.

"Okay, and you haven't heard from him at all?" Hyrum asked.

"No, and I've called his phone, it just goes straight to voice-mail. This isn't like him, Sheriff."

"And where were they going?" Hyrum asked.

"They were going to Delta to see a movie," Carol said, wiping her eyes with the tissue.

"Okay. Well, Mrs. Grains, he hasn't been missing for long enough to declare him a missing person yet," Hyrum said. Carol started to say something, her eyes going wide, but Hyrum brought his silencing finger into play. "But, I'll have Deputy Jensen take a drive down the road leading out of town and see if he can find your boy."

"I'm on it," Jensen said. He walked out of the office, leaving Lacey and Hyrum with Carol.

"Lacey, see if you can raise the Delta PD on the phone and see if they've seen the young couple?"

She nodded and walked back to her desk. Hyrum closed his notepad and put the pen back in his pocket. He led Carol back to the bench and sat down with her. She was still crying, but the intensity died down visibly.

"I wouldn't worry yet, I'm sure they are just fine. Maybe the storm delayed them, or they had car trouble. Deputy Jensen will find them. We'll call you when we hear something. Go home and get some rest."

Carol left the police building, leaving a trail of tissues in her wake. Hyrum sighed and got a wastebasket to clean them up. He washed his hands in the bathroom and was drying them when the radio buzzed with Deputy Jensen's voice.

"I've been driving this road for almost ten minutes. How far do you want me to go?"

Hyrum walked to Lacey's terminal and picked up the handset.

"Just go a little further, let me know if you see anything at all," Hyrum said.

"No problem, I'll just go anoth--"

The transmission cut off mid-sentence. Hyrum looked at the radio handset with a frown. After a moment he put it close to his mouth and hit the talk button.

"Charles? You there?" he asked.

Nothing but silence came back. Hyrum tried a couple more times but garnered the same results.

"What do you think?" Lacey asked.

"I don't know, maybe we lost power to a repeater or something. I'll go out and see if anything's wrong with the radio tower. It's the same way Charles went. Give Delta a call and let them know what's up."

"Sure thing, sheriff."

Hyrum drove out of town and followed the road that Charles would have been on. He drove past the radio tower, and everything looked fine. Hyrum tried to reach Charles again but to no avail. He kept driving down the road as he turned the bend, he slammed on the brakes and skidded to a stop.

He was right back at the edge of town

"What the hell?"

The acrid smell of burnt rubber and brakes punched into his nose. He flipped the car around and headed back out of town. Moments later, he found himself back in town. He tried three more times to no avail. Finally, he let out a growl and pushed the pedal all the way down to the floorboard. The Interceptor's speedometer climbed higher and higher until it buried the needle.

Telephone poles and fence-lines blurred as he raced down the county road. The radio tower came into view and he flew past it doing well over 120 miles per hour. Moments later he came upon the car's brake marks in the asphalt and the town of Elk Hollow loomed up to greet him. Once again he slammed on the brakes and fishtailed to a stop.

This time Marlene stood outside of the fuel station filling a basket full of apples. She shot him a look that mirrored the perplexed feeling that crept into his being. After a moment she waved at him. Unable to think of a different response, he returned the gesture.

There was a knock at the door. It started as a faint thump but quickly turned into a hammering crash as the door's assailant grew frustrated. Hyrum thrashed in his sheets for a moment and then rolled out of bed. His feet refused to find hold on the floor, and he stumbled into the dresser, knocking a nearly empty bottle of rum off the countertop.

The effects of the fallen bottle still swam through his veins, and the room pitched and rolled, much like the contents of his stomach. Hyrum took two more steps toward the front door, and then made a mad dash to the toilet. It had been over two years since he last drank, and even then, his last bender had been the night Zach died over twenty-four years ago.

Whoever stood outside knocking on his door certainly was tenacious. The constant knocking continued until he finished emptying his stomach in the bathroom, and stumbled through the living room.

"Just a damn minute!".

He fumbled with the deadbolt for a moment and then threw the door open. Bill Stoltz stood on his door, a dirty ball cap in one hand, his other balled into a fist, lifted in mid-strike. When the man noticed Hyrum standing there instead of an oak door, a cautious smile crept onto his face, partially hidden under a scraggly black beard.

"Mister Sheriff, sir?" Bill asked, enunciating each word as if spelling them out in his mind.

The image of Bill wavered for a moment, and the street in front of his house started to spin. Hyrum clutched onto the doorjamb and steadied himself. He shut his eyes until it felt like things had steadied, and then slowly opened one, and then the other. Hyrum raised his arm and looked at his watch, except his watch wasn't there, only bare skin.

"Bill, what do you want? It's," he looked to the imaginary watch again, "late."

"Mister Sheriff, sir? I th-th-thi-think, you ne-nee-need, to see th-th-this," Bill stammered.

Hyrum let out a sigh and almost lost control of his stomach again. The bile rose in his throat and burned his already tender esophagus. He forced the feeling down and leaned his head on his outstretched arm. What did he need to see? That nobody could leave town? He already knew that, try something else.

"See what, Bill?"

"Tra-trai-tra-train tracks, si-si-sir."

Hyrum looked up, and the world rolled again as if his house was a washing machine, and he stood trapped in spin cycle. He snapped his eyes shut. With the nightmares and the locals, Hyrum couldn't get a night's rest to save his life.

"What are you talking about? There aren't any train tracks in Elk Hollow. Did you lose what little brain you have left? Now I don't have time for games, I'm tired, and my insides are all jacked up."

Bill winced at each word as if they were a crack of a whip. Near the end, the man shied away, shivering.

Hyrum deflated. He let out another sigh and shook his head, hoping the motion would help clear his thoughts. All it did was cause his stomach to protest even more.

"I'm sorry, it's just been a shit day," Hyrum said, forcing his speech to come out softer.

Bill twisted his beat up hat. He shuffled on his feet in no particular direction and then pointed down the street.

"O-o-ov-over, the-the-there," Bill said.

Hyrum followed the direction the man pointed. The street lamp cast a pale white glow down to the road, but it didn't need to shine too bright. The tracks caught the light and winked at him from across the street.

"Who put those? When...?" Hyrum asked. When he got no response he turned back to Bill, but the man was shuffling off in the opposite direction of the tracks and up the road.

Even as drunk as Hyrum was, it only took him a couple minutes to throw his dirty clothes back on and stumble down the street. The train tracks glared at him, shiny and new. Pitch-black railroad ties sat anchored to the ground with polished, nickel-plated tracks. Golden spikes tacked the tracks to the ties. Horrible smelling gravel the color of raw meat covered the entire path. The smell reminded him of a mix of sewage and bad eggs and he couldn't help but vomit all over the shiny new railroad.

The tracks ran through the middle of town and stretched as far as he could see in either direction. There was no way someone could have built the tracks overnight without anyone noticing. No damn way.

Hyrum took out his cell phone and dialed into dispatch. An annoying beep-beep-beep spat from the phone's speaker, and when Hyrum looked down, he noticed he had no reception; in fact, he had no cell service at all.

He stumbled back to the house and tried the landline with the same results.

Hyrum found himself back in his bedroom, the bottle of rum staring at him from the floor. Drops of the amber liquid spilled onto the carpet, and even from where he stood, the strong odor of the drink punched him in the face. He picked the bottle up and emptied the last bits of the drink down his gullet, enjoying the burn as the rum raced into his stomach.

He grabbed his gun and badge from the kitchen table and went outside to his Interceptor. Hyrum flipped the radio on and called into dispatch.

"Lacey? You up? Hello?"

Static filled the car, and then a high-pitched squeal. Hyrum growled and flipped the radio off. He fished in his pockets until he found the keys.

He put the keys in the ignition and held them there for a moment. After a few minutes, he cursed and got out of the vehicle. He may have jumped back on the wagon, but he didn't have to add driving while intoxicated to his list of bad deeds.

Hyrum grabbed his coat from the hangar and a bottle of water from the fridge and then set off on foot toward the police station. The tracks ran in the same direction, so he followed the newly laid railroad, keeping far enough away in order to avoid the smell.

"Hyrum, I'm glad you're here; the world's gone to hell in a hand basket!" Lacey said.

He almost couldn't hear her from the clamor of the towns-people that crowded the small station. Over two dozen people filled the waiting room, and as soon as he walked through the doors, they turned on him, vying for attention.

"Sheriff! My wife's missing!"

"Hyrum, where did the railroad come from?"

"Sheriff, I can't leave town!"

"Is it terrorists?"

Soon it got so loud as the people tried to talk over one another that he couldn't make out what they said anymore. Hyrum held his hands up and motioned for them to calm down. It didn't work and they only grew louder.

"Shut up!" he yelled.

The crowd calmed down for a moment, but the levy didn't hold, and soon their voices poured out in force again. Hyrum threw his hands up in disgust and pushed his way through the wall of people. He made it to his office and slammed the door.

The mob's voice still carried through the thin walls, but at least it offered a small respite. He wiped the sweat from his brow and threw his coat into the corner of the office. A multitude of papers and folders occupied his desk, and he all but shoved them all off in order to make room to lay his head down. The headache was bad, worse than usual and Hyrum lamented his decision-making skills.

A small sticky note placed on the screen of his monitor caught his attention. Scrawled in his own chicken-scratch handwriting was the number to the local florist. A tremor started in his hands and his lungs constricted. He grabbed the note, crumpled it up, and threw it in the wastebasket.

Hyrum put his head back down, but the note stared at him from the trash bin. *Hyrum, we're going to be brothers forever, right?* He sighed and grabbed the phone. Nothing greeted his ears, no dial tone, no busy signal, nothing. His cell phone still showed no service.

"Damn it all!"

He threw the phone against the wall busting it into pieces and showering his office in various parts. The raging din of townsfolk grew louder for a second when his door opened. Lacey walked in and shut it behind her, holding her body against the cheap wooden portal as if the mob might rush through at any moment.

She looked at him wide-eyed, and then to the phone.

"You okay?" she asked.

"No, I'm not okay. Is anyone okay right now?" Hyrum asked.

She stared at him for a second.

"I can't make any calls," he said.

"Been like that all night. That's why these idiots are out there. I don't think I've taken so many missing person reports in my life," Lacey said. "And that railroad? What's going on Hyrum?"

Her voice was shaky and held that odd twinge telegraphing the onset of tears. Hyrum looked up from the desk and sat up a little straighter.

"I don't know, I really don't. I tried leaving town yesterday; probably a hundred times. I couldn't get much further than ten miles away before ending smack dab at the edge of the city."

"Me too," she said.

Those words beckoned the release of the held back tears, and when they started flowing, they ran like a swollen river after a storm. Lacey slid along the door and sat on the floor, her body trembling.

Hyrum got up from his desk and sat on the floor next to her. He took her shaking form into his arms and held her tight until she stopped shuddering. They stayed on the floor of his small office holding onto one another until the crowd dispersed from the other side of the doorway. When all was quiet, Hyrum stood up and helped her to her feet.

"Thank you," she whispered and wiped her face with the sleeve of her sweater.

He didn't say anything but nodded. Hyrum walked out and into the empty waiting area. Someone in the crowd must have gotten angry, because the potted plants lay destroyed on the ground, spilling their dirt across the gray carpet. The bench was overturned, and someone had stolen Lacey's computer monitor.

"Son of a bitch! Who'd take my computer? How am I going to take calls now?" she said.

"I wouldn't worry too much about it, nobody can take calls anyway," Hyrum said.

"I suppose, but still. What got into them?"

"I don't know."

Hyrum surveyed the wreckage, but something on the counter caught his eye. A blood red envelope with fine silver filigree sat directly under the illumination of the overhead canned lighting as if someone put the thing on display. Lacey followed his gaze and saw the card, and immediately walked over and picked it up.

"What is it?" Hyrum asked.

"I don't know, but it's addressed to me," she said.

She held the card out and showed it to Hyrum. On the front of the envelope, in the same color as the filigree, Lacey Grimes was written in elaborate cursive.

"Do you think it's an invitation to your uncle's funeral?" Hyrum asked.

"Uncle Edward? No, that was a couple weeks ago," Lacey replied.

"That's right, sorry. My mind isn't working properly right now," Hyrum said.

She opened the envelope and retrieved a thin card that was about four inches in length. Her hand started trembling and she dropped the envelope. She almost fell down when her knees buckled, but Hyrum caught her.

"What is it?" he asked.

She couldn't speak, so she just handed the paper over to Hyrum. He took it and helped her up before looking at what he now held—a train ticket for a departure from Elk Hollow two days from now.

The sun crept through the windows of the bedroom and planted itself on his face. He fought the urge to get out of bed. What was the point? Work wasn't an option anymore;

the phones were down, and the majority of people weren't in the mood for law enforcement. Before he left the station last night, more reports of missing people filled his desk. More people complained about not being able to leave town. Yet, worst of all, civility broke down quicker than he expected. The streets were filled with rampaging rednecks and delinquents. In fact, it wasn't the sunlight that finally urged him to move, it was the series of gunshots that erupted from across the street.

Hyrum rolled out of bed and snuck up to the window on his hands and knees. He grabbed his pistol from the nightstand and peeked out from the corner.

His neighbor, Jake Rawlins, stood outside wearing a bathrobe and flip-flops wielding a pump-action shotgun. A group of young teenagers ran in the opposite direction as fast as they could while the shotgun-toting man reloaded. One teenager wriggled in pain on the man's lawn, clutching his abdomen. He had to move, and he had to move quickly.

He stood up and raced to his front door. By the time he made it outside Jake had finished reloading and emptied the gun in the boy's face. Hyrum stood there, struck by the moment. The sheer brutality of the action paralyzed him and kept him rooted to the entryway.

His neighbor must have noticed because he looked up. He pointed back to his house with his gun.

"You see what those punk kids did?" the man asked.

Spray painted in bold red letters was the phrase *He waits deep in the mountain. He knows.* The freshly applied paint ran down from each letter like blood seeping from a wound.

"Why would they do that?" Jake asked, his voice cracking.

He dropped the shotgun and shuffled back to his house. Hyrum watched him, wondering what to do. So he pulled the hammer back on his weapon and pointed it toward Jake.

"Sto-stop!" Hyrum yelled.

Jake stopped at his front door. He looked down at his feet and crouched. Hyrum followed the man's movements with his gun, still trying to process the scene. Jake stood back up and had something in his hands.

"Stop!" Hyrum commanded. This time he stepped off his porch and into the street. "Bishop Rawlins put your hands up!"

His neighbor turned and held a red envelope up. The sun's rays hit the silver writing and lit up like a pinwheel of light.

"I just can't seem to escape it. Why can't I leave? My wife left. I was in the car with her but next thing I knew, I was standing at the edge of town! Why can't I go with her?"

Jake was on the verge of tears. He crumpled the envelope, threw it into the bushes, and turned to go back into his house.

"I can't let you go, Bishop. You shot that boy and I'm taking you in."

The words seemed to shock the man into the action. He whirled around and took three steps toward Hyrum. Hyrum reacted and pulled the trigger, and the gun belched fire. Jake stopped his advance and stared at the patch of grass where the bullet impacted, not two feet from where he stood. Hyrum shook with excitement and adrenaline, and then lowered the gun. In his entire career as a sheriff, he hadn't even pulled the gun out except to qualify at the shooting range.

Jake put his hands up and slowly backed up toward his house. When he neared his steps, he looked at his feet and slumped his shoulders. Jake sat down and picked up the red envelope, which was now in pristine condition and back on his front porch.

"I'm afraid it's too late. I don't think it matters anymore," Jake said. He put the envelope in his robe pocket and walked into his house. Before he shut the door, he turned once more towards Hyrum.

"I know why I'm damned. Do you?" Jake asked.

Hyrum's breathing sped up to the point that he had to sit down in the dew covered grass. *Hyrum, we're going to be brothers forever, right?*

"See you at the train station," Jake said.

Hyrum walked through the church's heavy doors into the large gathering hall. Pews lined both sides of the room, and a handful of people filled the seats; however, many went unoccupied. Sniffles and sobs filled the acoustics of the room like a depressing chorus.

His clothes reeked of alcohol and Old Spice, with a twinge of vomit. He found an empty pew and plopped down. Hyrum hadn't been to church in a few months, but for some reason, it felt like the only place left to try and find refuge. He folded his arms, closed his eyes, and dipped his head low. For the first time since his brother's death, he prayed.

No rays of divine light broke through the clouds and bathed him in His grace. No choir of angels sang their holy cadence and lifted him to salvation. The only thing he found was dark memories. Memories of an abusive father who drowned depression in alcohol, and exorcised rage with closed fists. Memories of his mother giving birth to his brother Zach and dying moments later from loss of blood. Memories of taking care of a severely handicapped and needy brother while he juggled high school, work, and making enough money to make ends meet. Memories of the night his brother died.

Hyrum, we're going to be brothers forever, right?

"Hyrum? Hyrum Woolley?" asked a soft voice behind him.

He turned in the pew and found the source of that soothing voice. A woman clutched a beat-up copy of the Book of Mormon in alabaster-hued hands. She wore a yellow summer dress that cascaded halfway down her legs but hugged her form in such a way that mesmerized him. Red hair shining like a setting sun rolled down her shoulders in waves and complimented the saddle of freckles on her face. Brilliant blue eyes lit up like stars when he turned.

"It is you Hyrum! Don't you remember me? Wendy, Wendy Barton."

Hyrum racked the file cabinets in his brain until he found the information, and then it came flooding back to him.

"Oh my god! Wendy? How? What are? I mean, when did you get back?" Hyrum stammered.

"A week ago. I came back to visit my mom," she said through a meek smile, suddenly nervous now that she spoke.

Hyrum glanced at her hand and noticed it was void of a ring. He turned back to her about to ask, his mouth open, but couldn't find the words.

"Divorced," she confirmed for him. "We got a divorce a month ago."

"I'm sorry to hear that," he said.

"Thanks," she replied.

She clutched the book a little tighter and hugged it to her chest. She had two orange sweatbands on her wrists that *almost* hid ragged scars. Hyrum narrowed his eyes, and Wendy put her hands behind her back.

"So, what's going on?" she asked.

"I honestly don't know. I wish I did."

She frowned and stuck her bottom lip out slightly. He watched her as she scanned the room, looking from pew to pew.

"So few of us left. I came back to visit my mom like I said, and to get away from him. It looks like I picked the wrong time for a visit," she said.

Her voice sounded like a songbird and he drank in the melody of it. Memories of high school and prom flooded back to him, and for the first time in a long time, he felt the edges of his mouth creep up into a genuine smile. Then reality forced its way back in.

"Look, you have to get out of town, and soon. I don't know what's going on, but I know it's coming to a head tomorrow morning," Hyrum said, standing up and lightly touching her shoulder.

Just touching her was almost too much and he had to draw his hand back. The smell of her skin almost brought him to tears.

"I can't," she said.

"You mean?"

"I can't leave. I tried. My mom, she got out."

Hyrum sat back down in a puddle of exhaustion and kicked the pew in front of him, eliciting an angry grumble from a man in a cowboy hat who sat nearby.

"What are you looking at?" Hyrum said.

The man grumbled something else but returned to his own business. Wendy came around and sat next to Hyrum. She sat very close and the feeling of her body near his calmed him. At least until he saw the train tracks in the crook of her elbow. Without thinking he ran a finger across them.

"I quit after I moved away. Then I met Greg," she whispered.

"Your husband?"

"Ex, but yeah. It was good for a bit, but good things never last. Things got," she looked away, "bad. Real bad."

Wendy adjusted the bands on her wrists and looked up at Hyrum. Her eyes were wide and pleading, but somewhere behind that wild look, lay a smidgen of hope.

"I thought maybe, because of all the bad things I'd done, that maybe I was damned! But when I saw you here. If you're still here, then I know there's still good people in this town."

Hyrum, we're going to be brothers forever, right?

He put an arm around her and brought her close. The scent of her hair filled his nostrils and he let it take him away.

They sat there for almost an hour, just enjoying each other's company. Finally, he found the words that eluded him.

"You've had some problems Wendy, but you aren't a bad person. I know you," he said.

"I am a bad person. I let the drugs take me, but worse than that, I enjoyed the hurt and the misery I brought on my dad when I stole his pain medication. I actually took physical pleasure when I heard him moaning."

She tensed when she said it, and Hyrum almost thought he saw her lips curl into a grin, but it passed so quick that he couldn't be sure.

"Your father was an evil man, Wendy, and the world was a better place when he finally passed on," Hyrum said.

"Like father like daughter I guess," she said.

Hyrum couldn't think of what to say, so he just held her tighter. Hyrum understood that people did strange things to the ones they loved. But sometimes it was for the better.

"Take me out of here please," she said.

"Okay," Hyrum replied.

Hyrum almost got a good night's sleep, but the gun blast from his bathroom ripped him from his slumber. He shot up and looked around in a panic.

"Wendy!" he cried.

He reached across the bed to shield her from whatever danger presented itself from the bathroom, but she wasn't there. Her side of the bed was still warm, and her scent floated on the air like a sweet smelling flower.

"Wendy?" he asked, a little louder.

Light from under the bathroom door plastered the bedroom walls with a dull glow. The glow illuminated Wendy's clothes piled on the floor, still lying where they had torn them off in a fit of passion. The dull roar of his shower played from the bathroom.

Hyrum got up and crept to the door. He placed his ear next to it and listened. Other than the running water, he couldn't hear anything else.

Hyrum reached out and opened the door. Steam from the shower rushed out and the humidity stuck to his skin. The smell of expended gunpowder stung his nostrils, as did the coppery stench of blood.

It looked like someone took a plate of meatballs and threw them against the dirtied white walls of the small bathroom. More blood pooled around Wendy's head, mixing with the color of her hair until they merged and became one and same.

A cry stuck in his throat and he fell to his knees. He knocked his service weapon from her lifeless hand and gathered her pale, naked figure close to his body. Hyrum sat on his cold, wet, bathroom floor rocking her dead form back and forth until the sun came up.

His legs tingled with a biting numbness when he stood. He used the sink as leverage to lift himself to his feet, and that's when he noticed the red envelope. Wendy's name glared back at him in silver writing.

He passed by a large group of people lined up near the railroad on his way to the cemetery. Some carried luggage, others simply stood in line with nothing but the clothes on their back. However, they all clutched a red envelope in their hands.

Lacey stood in the middle of the line, her hair disheveled and unkempt. She had a small carry on roller bag behind her. When Hyrum walked by, she waved meekly, but then looked back to the tracks, waiting. Blood dried on her white dress, and Hyrum didn't want to know where it came from.

Bishop Rawlins, still attired in his bathrobe and flip flops stood a little further ahead in line. He carried a black leather briefcase, but when Hyrum walked by, one of the latches came loose and the contents spilled out onto the ground. Hundreds of Polaroid pictures spewed into the road. The bishop scrambled to snatch them up, but the wind grabbed them and scattered them all about. One flitted close to Hyrum and he caught a glimpse of a boy tied to a cement post, wearing nothing but a dirty pair of underwear. Hyrum didn't get a good look, but he could have sworn that it was a picture of the Jefferson boy who went missing last year.

I know why I'm damned. Do you?

Hyrum continued walking as the Bishop tried to get his pictures back. Before Hyrum left the line behind him, he thought he saw a sprig of blood-red hair pass through the crowd. He turned to get a better look but didn't see what he wanted.

By the time he reached the cemetery, the sun blazed in the sky above him. Yet instead of washing away the darkness, it only served to beat down on him with oppressive heat. He ditched his coat next to a rectangular gravestone that jutted from the earth. Hyrum wiped the front of the marker clean and sat down. The tombstone read: *Zachary Timothy Woolley. 1985-1993. Brothers Forever.*

Hyrum pulled some of the weeds that sprouted up next to Zach's grave. When the area was clear, he sat back and stared at the grave. Finally, he cleared his throat.

"I'm sorry."

The very act ripped a sob from his core and he had to stop for a moment. He wiped his eyes clear and looked away.

"I just...I just couldn't do it. I'm so sorry."

He buried his head in his arms and rocked back and forth on the ground.

"Hyrum, we're going to be brothers forever, right? Aren't we?"

Hyrum flipped the switch to the compact oxygen machine that hummed next to his brother's bed. Zach's eyes widened when the flow of life-sustaining air ceased to feed into his lungs. Hyrum watched as Zach clawed at his throat and gasped for a breath. Zach reached for Hyrum, and his eyes asked why?

Hyrum couldn't take it anymore, so he walked away, only to return when he figured enough time passed. Hyrum found his brother on the floor, twisted in the cords and hoses of the oxygen machine. He flipped the machine back on and dialed 911.

"I'm sorry," he said.

A deep train whistle cut through the air and rattled his bones. The hairs on his neck and arms danced wildly and his lungs contracted in a small spasm. Hyrum looked back towards the train station and the bellowing whistle yelled once again. He turned back to Zach's grave, his lungs constricted even tighter, and he fought to calm his breathing.

A red envelope sat on top of the gravestone. Hyrum didn't need to look to know his name was on it.

The train's whistle cut through the air once again, letting everyone know it was time to board.

About the story: "All Aboard" appeared in the anthology, *Horror: Odd & Bizarre* published by Sirens Call Publications back in November of 2015. This story was a fun one to write and started with a, what if question. I asked myself: What if a set of railroad tracks appeared in a small town overnight? Throw in strange disappearances and the fact that the townsfolk were stuck in town, and it was great to explore the mental breakdown of the town's remaining populace.

"Damned"

A pril 17, 1912

We are damned.

I have delivered the world to Hell in a gift box of steel and steam. Both magnificent and opulent, the *RMS Titanic* was supposed to be the shining star of the fleet. Now it only serves as the Pale Horse of the Apocalypse.

I thought our luck in avoiding the iceberg two days ago to be a good sign. If I could go back now and change things, we would be sitting on the ocean floor—our secrets and horrors buried under tons of water and ice.

It started in Queenstown, our last stop for passengers before hitting the open sea. How I loved the ocean; its briny kisses lapping at my lips always brings a smile to my face. What I would give to die now in peace under the waves, instead of trapped like a rat in my quarters. I can hear them even now, banging and scratching at the door. At night it's the worst, but during the day they whisper. They beckon for me to come and join them, among other things I dare not retell. Devil be damned, they'll have to take me!

We picked up a strange pallet of cargo in Queenstown. Inconspicuous enough; a pallet of two wooden boxes, waist high, and both locked with a heavy duty padlock. Strange markings lined the lid of the boxes. Whoever put them there did so in a crude fashion. The markings consisted of a brown ink and lay sprawled on the wooden canvas in various swirls and slashes. It hurt my eyes to look for too long. They also stank. A mixture of putrid meat and stale water emanated from the crates.

The packaging list named various preserved specimens destined for Miskatonic University in Massachusetts. I reviewed the list for anything hazardous and found nothing. Just to be sure, I set my First Mate on the task to double check. The contents belonged to a Mr. Paul Henri Blanc who, according to the instructions, would be waiting for the crates in New York.

If only I had followed my gut feeling and cast those crates into the sea.

Things went as planned for the first two days of our voyage. Guests were entertained and awed by the spectacle of the ship, and the crew was happy to fall into their routine.

One of the deckhands, a short squat chap who went by the name of Stones, complained of strange noises in the cargo hold. I tried to imagine that perhaps we had a stowaway, or even that some of the guests had found their way into the hold. However, instinct screamed at me, warning of the boxes.

I ordered the First Mate to come with me, and together, along with Stones, we made our way to the cargo hold. The smell that awaited us in that hold brought back memories from the war. Once I visited a hospital while ashore and happened into one of the *darker* wards. It was a place of death and decay. That's what waited for us in the dark expanse of the hold–Hell's grim tyrant.

The fact that the mysterious cargo lay at the center of this new problem came as no surprise. What was a surprise was the scene that lay before us. Both boxes were broken open, and a mess of blood and pieces of what or who lay strewn about the floor next to the crates. A discarded pry-bar and broken padlock sat next to my feet, covered in offal and viscous fluid. When I knelt to examine the remains closer, I found pieces of cloth reminiscent of my crew's uniform.

The boxes themselves were empty, yet deep scratches and burn marks decorated the insides of each box. The stink of rotted meat permeated the wood of the crates.

After sprinting to the upper decks, I ordered the First Mate to put together a search. I wanted to know who was missing, and find what escaped the confines of the boxes. The cargo hold was to be sealed off to everyone with the exception of the First Mate and myself.

The wireless onboard was the best of its kind, and I intended to use it. I sent off a telegram to Mr. Blanc, wanting to know what was in the boxes, as well as a telegram back to the White Star offices informing them of the death of the crewman.

Our initial search found nothing regarding the contents of the infernal boxes; however, it did reveal the name of the dead man. The victim was one of the deckhands who helped load the crates into the hold. His name was Mathias Brandy, and according to his distraught brother, who also served aboard, he was a very religious man. According to his brother's telling, Mathias left that night muttering strange things with a wild look in his eyes.

The next day I received a reply from Mr. Blanc. It read as follows:

The boxes were not supposed to be opened! Make your peace with God, Captain. We are damned.

I sent a reply asking for clarification, but nothing came. It didn't matter. The truth of those words would hit home before too long. Damn the whispers! Damn the scratching! And damn them all to Hell!

More and more crewmen went missing, and even a few guests. We tried to keep it quiet, and tried to contain the situation, but it grew out of hand quickly. To add to the ever growing list of problems, we almost hit an iceberg. Quick maneuvering and all we lost was a little bit of steel plating on the starboard side. Yet as I mentioned before, it would have been better if we struck that ice head-on and sank to the depths.

Shortly after the incident, the truth revealed itself. Screams emanated from the dining saloon. What awaited us was Hell itself. A pair of creatures tore through the frightened guests with vicious efficiency. The things stood on furred goat legs, with a massive barbed tail swaying from their rear. Ruddy skin with patches of scale and scab ran up their torso, which connected to long, lanky arms. Their hands sported three fingers and thumb, capped with coal black talons that, from the evidence of the dead passengers, were capable of ripping through flesh and bone with ease. Yet it was the facial features that were the worst aspect. Death incarnate stared at me from across the saloon. Their skulls were elongated and slightly curved like a crescent moon. Barbed and twisted horns sprouted from their head and chins like some sort of deadly hair. Their eyes burned like bloody oranges which illuminated their visages.

I pulled a pistol from a hidden pocket in my coat and shot at one. The bullet went wide and splintered the chair next to one of the creatures. They both looked up at me and smiled in unison. Their mouths were full of horribly long, sharp teeth that dripped with the fresh blood of the passengers.

Words slithered into my head from nowhere and everywhere all at once. Their message boomed in my mind and threatened to deafen me with its infernal meaning. I couldn't understand the words, but I understood their intent—to dominate and destroy everything on this world.

Something that sounded vaguely like laughter filled the saloon. I lifted the pistol again and fired once more. This time the bullet struck true, and hit one of the creatures square in the chest. A gout of flame and glowing orange blood that looked like molten lava sprung from the wound. The nearby table burst into fire when the liquid touched it, but quickly died away to nothing. The thing continued to laugh.

I fired again and hit it in the face, stopping its horrible cackles. The thing dropped to the floor of the saloon and twitched. Its companion looked at its dead mate for a moment, and then turned its attention back to me. The thing snarled and raised its arms into the air and clenched its three-fingered hands into tight fists. It muttered something in its own language and once again my eardrums threatened to burst under the pressure.

What happened next sealed our fate. The dead passengers on the floor sprung to life. They all rose to their feet in unison, and I watched in horror as their bones snapped and rearranged themselves into some terrible mockery of the demonic creature. All at once, their expressions mimicked that of the demon's, and they smiled a macabre smile that threatened to leap off their faces.

They came at us then like crazed lunatics. Only I made it to the safety of my cabin. For the first few hours, I could hear the screams of the crew and passengers, as one by one they fell to the ferocity of those things. It wasn't much later that I heard the scratching, and then the whispering.

We should hit landfall soon in New York. When we do, the world is damned.

-Captain Edward J

About the story: "Damned" was my second published short story. It was published by Dark Moon Books in November of 2012 and appeared in their anthology, *Zombie Jesus and Other True Stories* (catchy title, right?).

I met the editors at a World Horror Convention in Salt Lake City earlier that year. I was working on the submission at the time, but it was going in a different direction. Instead of having the ship hit landfall, I had the ship sinking still. I remember asking the editors (nice folks by the way) a few questions, which re-directed the story. I'm glad I had that interaction or I'm sure my story would have made it to the rejection pile.

"The Scratch"

K evin pulled the magnetic key card from the reader and heard the heavy wooden door's lock disengage. The mechanical whirring noise only lasted a second, but it was a familiar sound to Kevin. He traveled a lot on business and had stayed in many motels. What wasn't familiar was the other noise heard as he pushed the door open. A scratching sound, like something was trying to get through a wall. It was loud enough to get Kevin's attention, stopping him dead in his tracks at the doorway.

His brow furrowed as he peered into the dark room. It was already after sunset, and the hotel wasn't high class enough to warrant a maid turning the sheets and leaving the light on. It was a departure from what he was used to, but because the Shakespearean Festival, as well as the First Annual Horror Writers' Association of the West convention was happening simultaneously, this motel was all he could find. He stared into the darkness and felt the hairs on his arm start to rise. He stood motionless, waiting for his eyes to adjust, listening for the noise to return. After a few moments he shrugged it off as nothing important and started to shuffle in.

Something scratched again across the wall in the far corner. Loud enough that Kevin could feel the vibration in the floor as whatever it was fell on the ground. Kevin dropped his luggage.

His hand fumbled across the wall searching nervously for the light switch.

Something blew across the nape of his neck as the light flared to life. Kevin spun around, tripping over his own feet. He scrambled back to get away from whatever was behind him. As he stumbled backward, he caught a glimpse of a dark figure in the doorway. His legs crashed into the coffee table, toppling the welcome book that had been so carefully placed there.

Kevin cried out in pain and looked back to where he had been standing. Nothing was there now. Just his luggage, a garment bag, a laptop case, and a small black roller case that had fallen forward, blocking the door from closing all the way. He got up and turned to face the room once more.

Every drawer, cabinet and cupboard in both the main room and the bathroom was open. The light began to flicker, raining a chaotic mix of light and dark into the room.

He stood transfixed, staring at the corner where the scraping noise had emanated from. He felt the sensation of someone blowing on his neck again and it pulled him from his stupor. He spun around. The lights stopped flickering just as the room's air conditioning kicked on and blew cool air into the room.

He went out into the hall and looked both ways. Nobody was there. He carefully weighed his options. He had an early morning meeting, and didn't want to drive all around town in the hopes of finding another vacancy. He finally decided he could take the potential rat in the wall, and faulty lighting for one night.

Kevin slumped his shoulders and let out a sigh. He grabbed his luggage and let the door close. He heard the comforting sound of the mechanical lock engage. It only took a moment to close all the drawers and cupboards. After kicking his shoes off and turning the television on, the strange series of events was all but forgotten. Perhaps the maid had left the drawers open.

Kevin felt a nice warm bath would help relax him. He kneeled next to the bathtub to turn the water on. Just before he twisted the old faucet, he heard the scratching noise again. He knew it was coming from the same corner as before.

He rushed into the main room. The television was on mute. It bathed the small room in a comforting pale blue glow. He flipped the lights on and moved closer to the corner.

He felt the temperature drop the closer he got. It was the corner closest to the window, but he couldn't feel a draft. It was the middle of June in Southern Utah and it wasn't cold outside.

Kevin crinkled his nose and gagged. The corner of the room smelled like a slaughterhouse, visceral and raw. He backed away, sitting onto the bed, its old spring mattress groaning in protest. He picked up the phone, his hands shaking slightly.

"Yes, Mr. Young?" a bored voice asked. It sounded tinny, like speaking through an old can and string toy.

Kevin looked at the phone in a mixture of confusion and disbelief. He hadn't yet dialed the front desk. Before he could respond, the voice spoke again.

"Mr. Young?" the voice inquired.

"Uh, yeah. I'm in room 1-"

"101 yes, I am very much aware Mr. Young. What can I do to help you?" the voice asked again with a hint of irritation.

Kevin felt his anger rising. He hated it when hotel workers, restaurant attendants, or any hired help took on an attitude, no matter how small.

"Look, there's something wrong with this room."

"I'm afraid I don't understand. Mr. Young I am no mind reader or visionary, you will have to use a little more description if I am to assist. Quit being such an idiot, Kevin."

He couldn't believe it. He had stayed in hundreds of different hotels, motels, inns, and hostels around the world, and he had never been confronted with such rude behavior. Not only that, but the phrase the man had used, *quit being such an idiot, Kevin,* was something his father used to say all the time. It brought back bad memories.

"Excuse me?" was all Kevin could muster.

The man on the other end of the phone let out an annoyed sigh.

"Mr. Young, I'm afraid I can't help you unless you explain the problem. Use your words."

Kevin snapped, his anger crushing his feelings of nervousness and fear.

"Look you little prick, I want to talk to your supervisor. This room is falling apart and something smells awful. It smells like-"

"Like something died Mr. Young? Yes, it smells like something was murdered. Torn to pieces and left in the corner for a week, doesn't it Mr. Young? Like something, or *someone*, had slowly died, *scratching* against the wall as it tried in vain to escape, its life slowly leaving its body. Is that what you smell Mr. Young? Like some *idiot* was killed in the corner?"

Kevin was speechless. The man's tone had turned from bored and irritated to spiteful and full of malice.

"Sleep tight, Mr. Young."

The line went dead.

He put the phone back on the cradle.

He wasn't used to being treated like that. Filled with rage, he pulled on a shirt on and stormed out of the room. He headed toward the reception desk, grinding his teeth together so hard that it hurt.

He arrived at the desk, looking around for the man who had lipped-off to him. He didn't see anyone. He scanned the front desk and his eyes focused on a small bell. He slammed the bell with his hand, its chime ringing into the lobby, cutting the silence like a razor. His anger had gotten the better of his patience and he hit the bell again, and again, and again.

"Okay, okay! Hold on," called a feminine voice from the back office.

A heavyset woman with blond hair came waddling out of the office. Her hair was up in curlers and she wore an oversized track suit, pink of course. She rolled up to the desk and snatched the still ringing bell from under Kevin's hand.

"I heard you the first time sir, is there something wrong?" she asked.

"Where is he?" Kevin all but yelled through gritted teeth.

"Who?"

"The man. I talked to a man on the phone just a second ago, and I have to say I am more than displeased. He was a damn prick and I want him fired! It was bad enough when the other woman took *forever* to check me in earlier, but this is ridiculous!"

"Sir, there's no need for such vulgarities. I'm the only one here. No one called the front desk, I can assure you."

He looked around, but he couldn't see anyone else. He hadn't passed anyone on his way to the desk, and his room was fairly close. His eyes narrowed and he locked the blonde giantess with a stare cold enough to make Scrooge want to put another coal on the fire.

"Are you sure no one was here?"

The woman slowly put the bell back on the desk, her small pudgy fingers leaving a smudge across its chrome surface.

"I am positive. I work the night shift, Maude works the morning, and Christina works the afternoons and evenings. We don't even employ a man at the desk."

Kevin slammed his fist on the hard wood of the desk causing the woman to jump. She let out a small cry of fright and took a step back. He looked up and saw her face, and his temper diminished slightly, replaced by embarrassment and a smidgen of guilt.

"I'm sorry, I don't mean to be an asshole, it's just I've had a long day, I'm under a tight schedule, and I am less than pleased with my room."

The woman's expression softened for a moment, and then her customer service training took over.

"Sir, I'm sorry about the accommodations. If I had another room, I would be more than happy to move you, but we're full up because of the convention. How about this, I can discount the price by 15%."

He let out a sigh and nodded in acquiescence. It was late, he still needed to bathe, and he had to be up in a few hours for the meeting. Looking for another motel was out of the question at this point. He decided he would speak to the hotel's upper management about the incident in the morning.

"Sorry again, and thank you. Just to let you know, there is some bad smell coming from the wall in the corner near the lamp."

"I'll have someone look at it first thing in the morning."

Kevin turned and started back to his room.

"Sleep tight," the woman said.

He stopped, a shiver ran up his spine as he spun around and looked back at her.

"What did you say?"

"I said, have a good night," she said smiling.

Kevin nodded once slowly as a cold hand gripped at his stomach. With a nervous look on his face, he returned to his room.

He opened the door to his room, the mechanical whir of the lock not as comforting as it had been earlier. The stress of the situation was getting to him, small noises in the hallway now made him jump, and he was constantly looking over his shoulder.

Thoughts of tomorrow's meeting kept creeping into his mind. It was a very important business deal at hand, one that would change his life. He was still unsure as to why he had to come all the way to Southern Utah to sign the document, but the buyer would not accept anything other than his physical presence at the signing. The buyer said something about having to see Kevin make the choice in person, about having to scratch his John Hancock on the dotted line.

He shut the door behind him and threw the deadbolt. He put the security chain up, and leaned his back against the heavy wood, letting out a sigh. He looked up, took one step, and stopped in his tracks.

All the drawers were open again.

His hands began to twitch, spasms involuntarily running from his fingers to his wrists. He wanted to move, his mind screamed for him to just open the door and leave, but his legs wouldn't respond.

The scratching noise started again from the corner as the lights flickered. Between the lights' violent dance, Kevin saw something moving in the corner. His hands shook uncontrollably. He looked down at them, eyes wide with fear. The tips of each finger were bloody and raw, and droplets of blood rained onto the blue carpet at his feet.

He tried to scream but his throat had constricted to the point that it hurt to breathe. He took a nervous step forward and his legs gave out, the muscles cramping. He fell to the floor, barely missing the coffee table he had crashed into earlier.

He propped himself up on his elbows and tried to push himself up, but his attention was drawn to the corner again. The lights flashed like a rave in full swing, making it hard to see clearly. There was definitely something in the corner. It looked like a hunched man, with his back to the room.

The man was naked and bloody with festering wounds cut down his back, as if he'd been whipped. Kevin could see he was shivering, whether from pain or the unnatural cold that had rolled through the room, he didn't know. The thing continued scratching at the wall, tearing skin and nail from his fingers, leaving blood streaked furrows in the drywall. Each scratch got louder and louder until Kevin's ears hurt.

Slowly, Kevin finally struggled to his feet. His hands had stopped twitching and he noticed that the blood had disappeared as well. He reached for the door handle and the lights stopped their fluttering and stayed on. The scratches continued, louder this time, and Kevin whirled to face the man in the corner.

There was nothing there. There was no sign of the man who had been crouched in the corner. Even the drawers had closed.

"Yeah. I don't think so," he whispered to himself. He started to open the door but the security chain stopped it. He tried again and again to force it open before he realized what the problem was. He shut the door and reached for the chain.

The phone rang.

It was a sickly, warbling tone.

It reminded Kevin of an old toy phone he had as a child that had run off batteries – when that phone was about to die, its death moan was similar.

He battled with thoughts of running from the room and answering the phone. Something about the phone pulled at his primeval senses. He had to answer it.

He inched toward the phone, avoiding the corner as best he could. The phone coughed another unsettling ring into the air and Kevin picked it up.

"Hello."

"Mr. Young, I am very sorry that you are disappointed with our accommodations."

It was the man again, his voice fading in and out. It sounded like he was talking through a malfunctioning bullhorn.

"What do you want?" Kevin asked.

"I want to personally come up there and help change your attitude toward our fine establishment. So many others have had that same room, and all have...found their stay very interesting."

Kevin slammed the phone down. It immediately started to ring again, this time with a slow wavering ring. He picked the phone up again.

"Mr. Young, I'm on my way."

Kevin pulled the phone from the wall, but he could still hear the tinny voice of the man on the other end. The sound scratched the inside of his skull.

He raised the phone above his head and smashed it on the ground, stomping the pieces until the man's voice finally disappeared. Cold washed through the room again, and the scraping noise started once more.

He looked to the damned corner and caught a glimpse of bloody hand reaching from the other side of the bed, clutching a handful of the bedspread and pulling. He jumped up as the bedspread slid onto the floor. He froze, unable to move.

Finally, he willed himself to hug the wall and slowly make his way to the door. As he rounded the corner of the bed, he saw the bedspread piled up on the floor like a shroud.

He rushed to the door and pulled the security chain loose. He turned the knob, but suddenly stopped and started patting his pockets.

"Damn!" he yelled.

He looked around frantically for his car keys. He ran to the coffee table and nearby sofa and started to upturn the sofa pillows. .

A sense of dread filled him as the lights started to flicker again. The broken phone came to life and he could hear the man's voice echo through the shattered mouthpiece.

"Mr. Young, I'm almost there to deal with you. There have been complaints of scratching coming from your room Mr. Young. You must be silent."

Kevin lost it. The keys were his salvation and he had to find them before the man came to his room. He searched every drawer and cupboard in the room, throwing them open with abandon. He chose the dresser near the cursed corner last. He flung the top drawer open and found it empty.

His hands started to spasm again. His eye twitched so fast it was hard to see clearly. He dropped to his hands and knees, looking for the keys. The lights were in full swing and he shivered in the corner.

He saw them under the bed. They had slid off with the comforter. He reached for the keys, his hand shaking violently. As his hand touched the cool metal of the key ring, the lights stopped.

"Mr. Young. Does it smell like something died in that corner?"

Kevin raised his head and looked to the door. His screams echoed down the hall.

Sergeant Folson closed the doors to the ambulance and slammed the palm of his hand against the window. Brake lights brightened for a moment then dimmed as the emergency vehicle started to pull away. Spinning blue and red lights cast their glow in the hotel's parking lot.

"Poor schmuck."

Folson turned and saw his partner finishing a cup of coffee. He nodded once and watched the ambulance turn into the street.

"You ever seen anything like that?"

Folson shook his head.

"Did you see him, crouched in the corner? I've seen a lot, but I've never seen a man scratch his name into the wall like that, he must of have done it over a thousand times. Plus, did you see his back? It's like some sort of animal clawed at him. What do you think got at him?"

"I don't know," Folson said shrugging his shoulders, "but it smelled like something died in there."

About the story: "The Scratch" was the first piece of writing I ever had published. It marked a huge milestone in my life and I can't tell you how stoked I was when I received my author copy in the mail. It was published by Dark Moon Books in their *Ghosts!* Anthology. Looking back at it, I'm not the biggest fan of this story anymore as I can see all sorts of things I would do different; however, I wanted to include it because it does hold a special place in my heart. Plus, I think many authors look back at their earlier works and cringe... it's all part of the process I suppose.

"The Devouring Maw"

Towering mesas of brilliant red stone and stunning vistas stretching farther than the eye could see greeted them at every turn as they made their drive to the trailhead. The landscape alone had made the trip worth it for Henry. However, if he knew what was to come, perhaps he would have opted to jerk the steering wheel and cause the small Geo Tracker to careen off the side of the cliff before they ever made one step up toward the hidden arch known as The Maw.

Henry's life-long friend, Danny, had insider knowledge of the place, which was supposedly nestled near the top of an old trail that didn't show up on any tourist brochures or guide maps. How Danny came about this knowledge should have been Henry's first indicator that things were not as they seemed. When questioned about the validity of said arch, Danny would say his sources were legit and that he had it on good authority that the arch was there. Apparently, these days, hearing something from your brother's girlfriend's great-grandfather who read it in an old journal was considered legit. Henry had his doubts, but he enjoyed hiking enough that it didn't matter if the arch was real or not. Besides, the name of the arch was enough to pique Henry's interest.

It was midday when they pulled off the highway and made the long trek up an unmarked dirt road. It was slow going, as the road hadn't been serviced since... well, since ever. Deep ruts cut through red clay soil winding around large rocks. After an hour, they arrived at a towering pine, long dead and nothing but a skeleton of sun-blasted wood reaching into the sky like a claw. Hanging from the bare branches were various animal skulls. The blank eye sockets of deer, elk, coyote, and cougar glared back at them.

Danny smiled and slapped the steering wheel. "Just like they said it would be. We're here!"

"This doesn't look like the start of a trail. It looks more like a warning," Henry said.

"What are ye', yeller?" Danny said doing his best Yosemite Sam impression.

"No, but I'm not stupid. I don't think we should go up there."

"Oh, come on, quit shitting your britches and man up. We've come a long way."

"Fine, but when we're being chased down the mountain by some sort of horrible creature, don't be surprised when I slap you with a big heap of I told you so."

The road ended at the trees, but there was a slight indentation in the dirt marking what looked to be a hiking trail winding up into a narrow canyon. Danny killed the engine and hopped out of the vehicle. Henry followed and was surprised when a cold wind rolled across his face. It was the middle of July in southern Utah, and cold winds shouldn't have arrived yet. The skies were clear, so it didn't look like a storm was coming.

The skulls clacked in the tree as the wind moved them, acting as a macabre wind chime. Other than the clacking, the only other sound was the click of the engine cooling. There were no other animals around.

"We follow the trail up, and it should lead us to The Maw. At least, I think it will."

"How far?"

"A couple miles. No big deal."

Sure, no big deal. The hanging skulls made it a big deal. The chilly wind whipping through the trees added to the big deal. The deal was big in Henry's mind. Real big.

Henry's stomach growled, and he realized he hadn't eaten anything since breakfast. He grabbed his daypack from the back of the Tracker and pulled a granola bar from one of the side pockets, devouring it in two big bites. After tightening the straps across his chest and arms, he took a big drink of water from the Camelback hose. It was a little warm but was nice running down his throat.

"Ready?" Danny asked.

Henry nodded and they started up the trail. Before hitting the canyon, he cast a quick glance back to the Tracker. All of the skulls in the tree had turned to watch them go, and the sight of all them staring back caused his heart to skip a beat.

"Hey..." Henry said, almost a mumble.

"What?"

The skulls turned in different directions until nothing looked odd at all. It must have been the wind.

"Never mind."

Two hours ticked by, but to Henry it was eons. Each step became harder to take and his stomach hurt he was so hungry. He'd already eaten all of his trail mix and the rest of his granola bars. He stopped for a moment to catch his breath and take a drink of water. The trail paralleled the ridge and gave him a view of the canyon floor below. A lazy stream the color of ruddy mud ran a thousand feet below them. He generally wasn't afraid of heights, but his legs turned wobbly and his vision tunneled.

Henry leaned back so the rough rocks of the mountain scraped his back. The solid surface gave him a small bit of comfort. He focused on his breathing, trying to bring his heart rate back down. As he took deliberate breaths in through his nose and out through his mouth, a squirrel scurried up to his foot and looked up inquisitively.

"Hello, little guy, how are you?"

The squirrel cocked its head and scampered up a dead pinion pine. Henry pulled his phone out of his pocket and got the camera ready to snap a picture. His girlfriend would get a kick out of the pic. Even though she didn't like hiking or camping, she loved animals.

He focused on the squirrel who stared back at him. The pic was going to be great. Just before he was able to snap a pic, there was a rush of wind, a blur in front of his camera, and then the squirrel was gone.

Henry looked up to see a hawk soaring away with the squirrel wriggling between its talons. It landed up the trail and began to devour the critter. He snapped a pic of the hawk eating its morsel and debated whether or not he should send the picture to his girlfriend when he got a signal again. She wouldn't appreciate the humor.

He snapped another pic. Then another. Henry zoomed in as close as he could and found the details came surprisingly clear. The hawk tore into the squirrel's body with a hungry fervor the likes of which he had never seen before in any nature documentaries. He supposed they wouldn't want to air footage that grisly, as the hawk's beak was covered in bits of fur and blood. His stomach complained, reminding him that he needed to eat as well, and for half a moment he wanted the squirrel to himself. Saliva built in his mouth as he thought about tearing the meat from its bones, picking it clean until there was nothing left.

Something grabbed his shoulder, and his feet slipped on the trail. He slid to his ass and almost went off the edge, but whatever had him by the shoulder pulled him back to his feet.

"Dude, you okay?" Danny asked.

Henry looked past his friend's wide-eyed expression to the hawk, but it wasn't there. Only the half-eaten corpse of the squirrel was on the rocks.

"Yeah, I'm fine. Just a little vertigo," Henry said.

"Let's keep moving; it can't be much further."

"Okay. Hey, do you have any food?"

Danny fished through his pack and handed Henry a package of jerky. Henry tore the bag open and ripped a piece of the dried meat between his teeth, imagining it was the squirrel. It only made him hungrier.

After another hour and a half, Henry stopped and sat on a large rock. "Hey man, you think we should turn back? The sun will be setting soon, and we have no idea how much longer it will be before we get to the arch."

Danny looked at Henry and then back up the trail. The trail twisted further up the mountain with no end in sight. There had been so many switchbacks and curves that if it hadn't been for the sun's position, Henry would have had no idea which way was north.

"No, let's keep going. I mean, say it gets dark. We can continue to push on, or hell, I'm sure we could find a spot flat enough to sleep the night through. You don't have anything you need to be to tomorrow, right?"

"That's not the point. I mean, we're chasing after an arch that may not be real, and I'm starving. I've already eaten all my food and yours. Let's just go back. I don't even want to see the arch anymore."

Just talking about food made the hunger pangs worse. His stomach roared for sustenance, and Henry thought about going back to eat the dead squirrel.

"Come on, we're so close!"

"Are we? Do you even know where we are? I'm all for adventure, but enough is enough. I'm heading back."

Henry turned and headed back down the trail. He let out a small smile of victory when Danny's footsteps crunched behind him.

"Fine, have it your way," Danny said.

They started the trek down the mountain, but after another hour, they came to a small plateau with a ring of dead pines surrounding it. Henry stopped and his heart started racing.

"What the hell? This wasn't here before!" Henry said.

He looked to Danny, but his friend remained silent, staring at the trees with a glazed look. Danny opened his mouth to say something, but the words must have gotten lost along the way.

Henry turned to look back up the trail where they had just come from, but when he did, the world spun worse than any drunken bender he'd ever experienced. He almost threw up and had to take a knee to keep himself from falling over. When everything stopped spinning, he noticed that he was looking *down* the trail, not up it. Somehow, they had gotten spun around and had been going up, instead of down.

"What in the hell? What in the holy hell?" Henry asked.

"May-maybe we took a wrong turn," Danny said. "Should have taken a left at Albuquerque."

Danny chuckled.

"Really? You think this is funny? We're lost on a trail that should be easier to navigate than a backcountry road and you're laughing?"

Danny's chuckle turned into a full-on laugh. Henry grabbed him by the backpack straps, ready to throw him to the ground and pummel him.

Rip his flesh and chew on the gristle.

However, when he grabbed him, tears were streaming down Danny's face, cutting muddy paths through the dust on his cheeks. Danny's eyes were wide and bloodshot, and he continued to stare at the ring of trees as if Henry wasn't even there. The man continued to laugh.

Snap the bones, suck out the marrow.

Henry shook Danny hard, and the glazed look disappeared from his friend's eyes, replaced with fear.

"Snap the bones..." Danny whispered.

"What? What did you say?"

Danny's brow furrowed. "I didn't say anything."

Henry let him go and crept over to the edge of the plateau. They were above the clouds, and he couldn't see the bottom of the canyon anymore. There was a smoky haze around them, blocking out the sun and casting the sky in a brilliant palette of orange, red, and pink. For a moment, there were two great orbs blazing in the sky, twin suns. Henry wiped the sweat from his brow and blinked away the grime, and the second sun disappeared.

"We shouldn't be here," Henry said.

"No shit, Sherlock."

"No. I mean we shouldn't have come here. There's something terribly wrong with this place. It's as if everything is, I don't know, off a little."

"What are you talking about?" Danny asked.

"Can't you feel it? I can feel it in my—"

Bones... delicious bones.

The temperature dropped, and the wind picked up. The clouds overhead roiled and rolled, turning from the brilliant colors to a dark and sickly grey.

"Come on," Henry said.

Danny didn't need any prodding. They'd been caught in mountain storms before and both knew they were no laughing matter. They needed to find cover. Henry led them up the trail and through the circle of dead trees. There was a flat rock in the middle with odd carvings that looked like runes lining the edges. A rusty stain splayed across the top of the rock, and Henry didn't want to know if it was really blood or not.

Blood. Tasty and salty.

The trail continued up for about a quarter mile leading to what looked like the mouth of a cave. The storm was getting worse, with lighting inching closer and closer with each flash. Thunder rumbled so loud it shook Henry's core.

"Hurry!" Henry yelled, but his voice was lost in the wind.

As they neared the top, the trail narrowed until there was only room for one of them at a time as the mountain rocks sloped up in a V on either side. The cave opened up before them and Henry wasted no time getting out of the storm. Once inside, he turned to find a storm whipping the mountain in a frenzy. The winds blew dust, rocks, and debris every which way, and it was hard to see more than a few feet from the entrance.

"Thank god for this cave," Danny said.

"Yeah. Sure," Henry said under his breath.

The cave stretched out before them. With the storm blocking the rest of the setting sun, it was impossible to see how far back the cave went, but something told Henry it stretched on forever.

Henry fished his headlamp out of his pack and clicked the light on. The bright LED bulbs flared to life and illuminated the cavern walls.

Old pictographs decorated the walls, depicting all manner of scenes. There were dozens of different animals drawn, from deer and wolves to elk and bear. Some of the scenes showed mountain lions eating other animals and what looked to be people. Another scene depicted a strange horned creature that looked like a possible bear with elk antlers attacking a group of humans.

"Henry?"

He continued down the cavern, following the pictographs. The scenes became stranger and stranger. The pictographs continued down the wall showing a drawing of a large stone archway. Through the arch, there were two circles with a fire burning around them. Twin suns.

"Henry?"

Humans hunted animals, piling them up and setting them afire. Horrifying (*delectable)* scenes. They showed people hunting down and eating animals. People eating other people (*the marbled meat is to die for).*

"Henry!"

There were crude images of men, women, and children being devoured by something. He couldn't tell exactly what it was, but it looked like a mountain with hundreds of mouths, all filled with long teeth.

Vorasker. Devourer.

Danny grabbed him by the shoulder and spun him around until Danny's headlamp shined him in the eyes.

"What?" Henry asked.

Danny pointed. Near the entrance was a small fire pit with a stack of wood, neatly piled.

"What the hell is up with that?" he asked.

"I don't know," Henry said.

"Why would there be a firepit and wood ready to go? Who the hell put it there?"

"I don't know. But you'll be damned sure that I won't let it go to waste. I'm freezing my ass off," Henry said.

Before he could move, there was a loud whistle from further back in the cave followed by a gust of foul-smelling wind.

"What the hell?"

"I don't know," Henry said.

"We need to go."

"We can't, not with the storm outside. Let's just get the fire going, and hopefully it will keep the animals away, if that's what it is."

They got a fire going easy enough, and soon the warm crackle of the flames kept the storm's chill at bay. As the fire swayed, shadows danced across the rock walls as if the pictographs danced along with them. Hopefully, the storm would blow over soon and they could get the hell off the mountain.

Danny was quiet and sat with his legs curled up to his chest, staring into the flames. Every now and then, another whistle would start from further back in the cave followed by another foul blast of wind as if something was dead back there in the dark. Dead and waiting.

Dead and delicious.

As the night wore on, Henry's eyelids grew heavier. The stress of the day and their situation bore down upon him, and he found it harder and harder to stay awake.

"Hey man, we should take turns getting some shut-eye. We're going to need our strength in the morning to get back down the trail," Henry said.

Danny's response was a light snoring.

"I guess I'll take first watch."

He took some measure of comfort in Danny's snoring. It was a bit of normal he could latch onto in the sea of crazy. Before too long, Henry's head started to bob. He moved over to wake Danny up to take his turn at the watch when something scraped across the rock in the darkness of the cave.

Henry stopped and listened.

He was about to write it off as nerves and an overactive imagination when it happened again, closer this time.

Henry grabbed Danny's leg and shook it. Danny groaned and kicked out.

"Wake up," Henry said through his teeth.

"Just a bit longer."

Henry punched Danny in the thigh.

"Ow! What the hell, man?"

Henry put a finger to his lips and pointed back into the cave.

"There's something in here with us," Henry whispered.

They listened, but there was nothing but the soft howl of the wind and crackling of the fire.

"Man, you need to get some slee—"

Two steps echoed off the cavern wall.

"Who's there?" Henry asked.

There was another step followed by something stumbling towards them. Henry tried to click his headlamp on, but his hands were shaking too badly. The steps picked up in speed until it was running at them.

Danny scrambled to his feet, and Henry tried to get up but fell over backward. He caught a glimpse of something rushing from the darkness. He couldn't see much, but it had a wide-open mouth. The fire blew out as another gust of wind came from within the cave, covering everything in darkness. That's when the screaming started.

Henry woke to find himself lying on the hard ground. It was completely dark, and he couldn't see anything other than the red glow from some coals. He turned on his headlamp. Danny was gone.

"Danny? Where are you?"

Nothing.

Henry stood, groaning as his body protested the movement. There was a slight sting on his head, and he winced when he reached up and touched the sensitive spot. His hand came away with a bit of blood.

Blood is good. It makes the meat juicy.

"Danny?"

There was no response, but his light caught something reflective deeper in the cave. He made his way there and found Danny's backpack on the ground. It was sitting in a pool of blood.

"Danny!?"

A trail of blood led further back as if something or someone had been dragged along the floor. Henry followed the trail, using the cavern wall to steady himself.

He kept going until he ran out of breath. Henry kept his light shining down the cavern, hoping to catch a glimpse of his friend, but it was nothing but rock and darkness.

The whistle came again along with the rotten stench. This time, it was louder, and the smell was stronger. Whatever it was, it was close.

Henry pressed on until he rounded a corner. He had found The Maw.

The cavern opened exposing a starry sky. Nestled under a rock wall was a massive arch with stalactites spiraling down from the inside like crooked teeth. A pile of bones and carcasses lay at the base, and the stink of rotten meat hit Henry's nostrils, causing him to retch. The wind picked up from outside and blew through the arch, making the whistling noise that had haunted him before. The closer he got, the more the wind sounded like screaming.

Henry inched his way closer to The Maw—closer to the pile of dead things.

Delicious things.

His stomach rumbled, and he couldn't help but drool as his mouth watered. He was hungry. The hunger dominated his thoughts. He wanted meat. Savory, juicy, bloody meat.

The ground trembled under his feet, bouncing stones around the dirt covered floor and shaking dust from above. As the earth shook, the view from inside the arch shifted slightly like a television losing a signal. The image skipped from the starry sky to a sun-blasted wasteland with two suns burning hot in the distance. The heat wafted through the arch, warming his skin. The temperature was nice at first, but the closer he got, the more intense it became.

He stood at the base of the bones. They rose high above, dwarfing him. There were animals but also humans mixed into the mountain of skeletons. Skulls of people long dead grinned back at him with broken teeth and empty sockets. There were other things in the bones as well. Skeletons of great creatures he couldn't recognize with elongated talons, wings, and teeth that still looked razor sharp. Curved horns protruded from the skulls similar to that of a ram, curling around in a circle. There were tall creatures with no eye sockets at all, yet to Henry, they still stared at him, waiting.

A quiet moan came from the top of the pile.

"Danny?"

The moan became louder.

"I'm coming!"

Coming to devour.

Henry started to climb up the pile. It was hard going, as the bones constantly shifted under his weight. He got on all fours and crawled higher when he could no longer walk. Henry reached up, and white-hot pain blazed through his hand as his finger bone snapped. He pulled, but something had a hold of his finger, and any movement caused the pain to burn hotter than before. There was a sickening crunch, and his hand was free. Blood poured from a stump where his index finger should have been. Above him was a bloody skull.

The snapping of thousands of mouths echoed through the cavern. The pile began to shift underneath him, and the clacking of jaws became louder.

Danny's moaning escalated into screaming.

Henry scrambled up the pile, but the skulls bit him, ripping his clothes and flesh alike with each agonizing inch upward. The heat coming from the arch grew hotter and hotter as he continued up, and his skin began to blister. The pain penetrated throughout his body, causing his eyes to water. He wanted to throw up and almost did whenever he brushed his finger stump across anything. Each time he hit his hand on a piece of bone, agony flashed up his arm.

He was near the top. Danny lay on top of the bones at the threshold of the arch. He was covered in blood, and his breathing was shallow and ragged.

Marinating.

Henry crested the last skeleton and crawled over to Danny. He reached out and grabbed Danny's hand. His friend's grasp was weak, but at least he was still alive.

"Come on, we're getting out of here," Henry said.

Danny mumbled something, but only a bubble of blood came from his lips. Henry got to his knees and tried to figure out the best way to get them both down without killing themselves. Danny was a mess, covered in dozens of cuts and scrapes.

Tenderized.

His stomach rumbled, and the hunger washed over him. The meat on Danny's neck glistened under the weight of the two suns. Henry reached out with a shaky hand. He didn't know how he would stop the bleeding...

...tear the flesh...

...there was so much blood. The air was thick with its coppery scent.

Irresistible.

Henry placed his hands on Danny's chest. He still had a heartbeat, but it was very faint. There was a small cut next to his upper ribcage. Lifeblood seeped from the wound. Henry moved his hand to the blood and let out a slight chuckle when it poured over his fingers.

He grabbed a flap of Danny's skin and pulled ever so slightly. Danny moaned in pain and tried to slap Henry's hand away but lacked the strength. Henry, pulled harder, ripping the wound and tearing a morsel of flesh off.

Danny screamed and tried to roll away, but Henry pushed down with his good hand, keeping him in place.

Danny's scream drowned out to nothing as a ringing started in Henry's ears. The ringing became louder until everything else came in a muffle. The roaring of the stomach matched the ring in his ears, and he couldn't think of anything other than the piece of meat in his hand. Blood and gore dripped onto his finger stump, but instead of hurting, it felt... good.

Henry's heart beat faster as he inched the bit of Danny's flesh to his mouth.

Eat it.

He opened his maw and placed the meat onto his tongue. The juices flowed down his throat. They were warm, but they felt nice. He chewed on the flesh, savoring each time his teeth ground the meat. Then, he swallowed.

There's more where that came from.

A wave of pleasure trembled through his core and he let out a sigh. Drool rolled down his chin and dripped to the bones beneath him.

Henry looked down to Danny. His friend was sobbing and trying to roll away. Henry grabbed him by the legs and pulled him close. His hand tingled, but the pain was dulled under the euphoria he was feeling.

"Please, don't," Danny croaked.

"Shhh, don't fight it. It will be okay. It will be... delicious."

Henry pulled him closer and bit into Danny's neck. Blood sprayed into Henry's face as his teeth broke through Danny's jugular vein. Danny kicked and fought, but after a few seconds, he lay still.

Henry tore a chunk of flesh off and began to gnaw on it. He wanted more. Even though his mouth was full, he rushed to pull more meat from Danny's lifeless body.

The bones shifted under his weight. He tried to stand and get away, but his feet were sinking. Something had a hold of his legs. The more he fought to free himself, the tighter the grip became. Then, it jerked him down. He sank to his waist.

Henry screamed and tried to find a handhold, but everything was just loose bones and rock. The thing jerked him again, and he sank to his chest.

"No! Help!"

He tried to grab the arch but knocked his severed finger stump across the rough rock. Pain lanced up his arm, and he saw stars for a moment. Then, something grabbed his arms and pulled him even further down. Only his face was above the bones.

He screamed again and then was pulled completely under.

Devoured.

Henry woke at the base of the bone pile. His body was ripped, torn, and bleeding from several wounds. His vision was blurred, and pain unlike he had ever experienced rolled through his broken frame. Something else was inside him. A hunger that overcame all the pain. He wanted to—*needed* to—eat, or the pain would only grow worse.

He got to his feet. There was a scent coming from the entrance of the cave, something that smelled *delicious.*

He stumbled toward the scent, sniffing in the darkness, a dog trying to find its buried bone. Henry tripped on a rock and slid to his knees. He crawled, moving closer and closer to his goal.

As he rounded the corner, firelight greeted him. The light stung his eyes, causing them to tear up. The scent was strong, and it overtook his senses. He needed to find the source and chew it, rip it, tear it.

Now there were voices coming from the fire. Two shadowy figures sat near it, staring back at him. He could almost taste the meat. Bloody and raw.

He stood, took a step, and stumbled. The voices grew excited, but he couldn't understand the words. He tasted their fear though, and it was enough to send him over the edge.

Henry ran toward the pair with his hands outstretched. A wind kicked up behind him, blowing out the fire, and for half a second, it looked like one of the shadowy figures was Danny. It didn't matter. Henry was hungry. That's when the screaming started.

About the story: "The Devouring Maw" was published by Twisted Tree Press and appeared in their anthology, *Hunger*

in April of 2018. This tale indirectly connects with an un-named project I'm working as well as my Dark Tyrant Series. How, you ask? Well perhaps that portal goes to a place where Euniphrites came from. Not familiar with the Euniphrites? Then perhaps you may want to check out the book, *Conse-quence*. Basically, they are demonic creatures from another world that wreak all sorts of havoc and destruction wherever they go.

"The Dark Place"

The clouds churned above Rosa, threatening to release another torrent of rain at any moment. The storm had come upon her without much warning. One moment it had been sunny and warm, the next dark and gray, with thunder bellowing all around her.

Rosa picked up a rock from the ground. It was still wet from the recent rains and leeched what little warmth was left from her skin, but it was real. She was sure of it... well, mostly sure. She had lost her pills when crossing the river. At first things were fine, but as the days turned into weeks, things were getting fuzzier. Since getting separated from Mama, things were getting worse.

They are coming, mija! Run! I'll lead them away!

That was two days ago. Mama didn't show up at the big tree that looked like a skeleton. That had always been the plan since hitting the mountains. Meet at the skeleton tree. The man with the big beard and soft eyes marked it on their map. It was supposed to have supplies. It didn't have anything but a gym bag full of empty protein bar wrappers. Ever since the rain, it was getting colder and colder, and Rosa couldn't wait anymore.

Mama wasn't coming back; however, *they* were coming. The falling temperatures told her that much.

They bring the cold with them, mija.

She had to find somewhere to hide and somewhere to get warm again. Otherwise, she'd freeze to death before *they* or anyone else ever found her.

She had spied the cabin from below, its green metal roof catching a lone ray of sun. It was as if God himself had given her a sign. The hike up had her huffing and puffing for air, and the dirt road was slick with mud. Yet, she found it.

The cabin was two stories tall. The number two was carved into a sign near the door. Rosa bounced the rock in her hand before sending it through the cabin's window. The noise startled a nearby bird and it flew off with a caw.

The wilderness fell silent as the bird retreated to another part of the forest, a part that didn't involve rocks hitting windows. Rosa listened, trying not to breathe. Had *they* heard? She prayed they hadn't and unlatched the lock on the broken window and crawled into the cabin.

She found herself in a small kitchen and immediately opened up the fridge and cupboards. The fridge was empty and turned off, and the cupboards only held a handful of cooking implements and seasonings. Rosa's stomach growled, dejected.

She turned on the faucet to the sink and pipes rattled, yet surprisingly water began to pour. Rosa leaned over and drank up the water. It had a strange, metallic taste, but she was thirsty and didn't think much of it.

A branch snapped outside, louder than a gunshot. Rosa turned off the water and sunk down onto the floor.

They had heard her break the window, she knew it. Rosa held her breath and closed her eyes, hoping they would move on.

Be careful, mija, for if they get you, they'll take you away to a dark place. A place where you'll be lost. They'll take you away and you'll never be found again!

Rosa didn't want them to take her away to a dark place. Her mother's words had scarred her from an early age, and ever since her mother first uttered them, Rosa had looked over her shoulder, always on the lookout for *them*.

What are they, Mama?

Demons, mija. Demons. They bring the cold and darkness with them. As cold as ice.

There was a creak from the boardwalk that was beside the house. Rosa stifled a scream and bit into her hand. Tears ran down her cheeks, and her heart felt as if it would tear through her chest.

Rosa shivered, and her breath formed small clouds of condensation in front of her face. Another sign they were close.

They suck your will to live, draining you of everything decent until you're just a thing, no longer a person. You'll change when they take you, until one day, you're discarded, or even worse, mija—you turn into one of them.

Rosa crawled toward the hallway. The hard floor sent waves of pain bouncing through her knees as she scuttled across the fake hardwood. Rosa scurried past the main entrance but stopped.

The door rattled as if something was trying to force its way in.

The wind outside picked up, and thunder boomed in the distance. Lightning flashed and sent shadows dancing all across the wall. Shadows that moved like people, but not. Shadows that encroached ever closer to Rosa.

She got up and ran up the stairs.

Stupid.

The wind howled and sent something crashing in the kitchen below.

The door shook along with the entire cabin. She was sure they would break in at any moment and come take her away to the dark place. Upstairs there was a hallway with a room on either end. In the middle of the hallway, facing the stairs, there was a tiny door about a quarter of the size of a normal door. A small end table was slid up against it, and there was a handwritten sign that read: Do Not Open.

A window broke downstairs, and Rosa let out a scream. She ran into one of the bedrooms. It was a simple layout with a bed with folded linen stacked on top of the mattress, a cheap wooden nightstand, and a chair upholstered in an ugly floral print that smelled like a retirement home. She closed the door behind her and slid the chair over to block the entrance. It was dumb but better than nothing.

Rosa pulled a blanket off the pile and crawled under the bed. She covered herself with the blanket and waited.

The wind screamed and the cabin shook. Thunder boomed across the mountaintops, and the lightning created a light-show throughout the room.

They come like a storm, mija. Lights rolling like lightning across the sky. They make noise everywhere they go, because they don't care... By the time you hear them, it's already too late.

They never came upstairs, or if they had, Rosa never knew. She woke up underneath the bed, wrapped in the blanket. Drool ran from the corner of her mouth and had pooled on the floor. She lifted her head and bumped it against the metal frame of the bed.

"Ay, Dios mio!" she said and slid out from under the frame. Her head throbbed, and every muscle in her body protested as she stood.

Rosa tiptoed to the window and peeked out. The sun shined brightly across the valley below and the winds had died down to a slight breeze that tickled the aspen trees.

She listened as hard as she could, but the cabin was silent. Perhaps *they* couldn't find her, so they left? Rosa opened the door to the bedroom and winced when the hinges let out a long squeak.

As she walked past the small door, a cool draft blew from underneath, lightly touching her exposed ankle. The sensation caused her skin to break out in goosebumps, and she shivered. Rosa would have to remember to give that door a wide berth. There was something about it... She couldn't quite figure it out. Perhaps it was the way it was blocked off? Or maybe the note saying not to open it... Something she didn't like. Or maybe it was because she knew that behind that door was a dark place.

They will come to take you away to a dark place.

Rosa hurried down the stairs and found the cause of the crash from earlier. A tree had fallen during the storm and broken the large window above the couch. Shards of glass littered the floor, catching the sunlight in a hundred different ways. It should have been a beautiful sight, instead, it only sent waves of pain through her head.

Her mouth was dry, so Rosa walked over to the sink and turned it on. The pipes rattled again, but there was another noise, a knocking. She took a quick drink and then turned off the faucet, but the knocking continued. A few small raps, then quiet. It came again in rapid succession. Then it stopped.

Rosa walked toward the front door. She reached for the doorknob when the knocking happened again. She froze.

It hadn't come from the front door but from upstairs. Rosa climbed the stairs, her eyes locked on the small door that looked bigger than before, almost towering. However, when she stood in front of it, it only came up to her chest.

"H-hello?"

Only silence and the note: Do Not Open.

When they take you to the dark place, mija, you can't see anymore. After a while, you lose count of how many days you've been in there. All you see is the others. The others they have taken. Others like you.

The knocking happened again. Quick thuds against the wooden door. The knob shook with the knocks, and Rosa fell backward and almost toppled back down the stairs.

They were here. *They* were coming for her.

Rosa scrambled to her feet and ran down the stairs.

"Mija, stop!"

It was Mama's voice, and it was coming from behind the tiny door.

"Mama?"

"Sí, it's me. Can you help me?"

Her mother's voice was soft, muffled. As if she were further away. Rosa climbed the stairs until she found herself in front of the door again. There were noises from downstairs, but she couldn't focus on those. They faded into the background, almost like a buzzing. Voices too, but she didn't listen. Her ears were tuned to her mother's voice.

"Mama, how did you get in there?" Rosa asked.

"Open the door. It's so dark in here."

Rosa moved her hand toward the knob but hesitated. Do Not Open.

"I... I don't know. I'm scared, Mama."

The cool air caressed her skin from underneath the door, and the knocking happened again, more distant than before.

"I know you are, mija. I'm scared too. It's so dark. I can't see anything. You have to help!"

Tears rolled down Rosa's cheeks and blurred her vision. She reached out towards the door. From downstairs came a crash as something busted into the cabin. Footsteps pounded from below, but Rosa didn't care. Her mother was in trouble, and only she could help.

She grabbed the wooden table. It was heavy and hard to move across the floor and squealed as she forced it away from the door. Rosa turned the knob and cracked the door open, peering into the darkness.

There were a few small holes in the wall, and sunlight tried to creep in the small room, but the shadows were able to keep the light at bay. Rosa couldn't see anything.

"Mama?"

Something moved in the corner, scratching against the wood. Rosa turned toward it just as something small and white flew past her. She screamed and threw her arms up over her face as the *thing* hit her then fluttered away. Rosa tried to see what it was, but it had already flown downstairs before she could get a good glimpse. She hoped it was just a bird. It had to have been a bird.

Rosa got to her knees and started to dust herself off when something else moved into the small room. A slight creak of the floorboards followed by a crack that sounded like bones grinding together.

The voices in her head were getting louder. Something was coming up the stairs, but she didn't pay it any attention. Instead, her gaze was transfixed in the darkness and the two pinpoints of light that had just blinked at her. Eyes like those of a cat at night.

Rosa wanted to move. She wanted to run as far and as fast as she could, but she was frozen. Her legs refused to budge other than to tremble in rhythm with her heart.

"*Mija, is that you?*"

The voice was death, littered with rot and decay—gravel against wet sand. There were more pops and cracks as the thing in the darkness moved. The eyes came closer.

"*Come... Help me out of here.*"

From the dark room, a hand emerged. It grasped the door-frame with gnarled fingers the color of birch bark and dirt. Bones ground against each other as the hand grasped the wood, crackling through the air. Long nails extended like talons and dug trenches into the wall.

Rosa took a step back, her legs finally able to move.

"*Don't go, mija. Come in here and HELP ME!*"

Rosa turned and ran down the stairs. The thing scrambled across the hardwood floor above her, its nails clacking as it came after her. Rosa turned the corner too fast and stumbled down the last flight. She got to her feet and wobbled towards the door.

"Mija! Come join me and the others in the darkness! Don't go!"

Rosa glanced back and instantly wished she hadn't. The thing stood on the landing and pointed at her. Its mouth was large, larger than any person's should be. Long limbs stretched towards the ground, and it had twisted, greasy hair the color of burnt coal.

Rosa screamed and ran toward the door but ran into something solid. She fell back on her butt and scrambled back on her hands and feet. Standing before were six figures with solid black eyes draped in matching shrouds of ice.

They had found her.

About the story: "The Dark Place" appeared in the anthology, *Peaks of Madness*, published by 42 Books in April of 2019. It was an anthology put together by the Utah Chapter of the Horror Writers Association (Note: there was no sponsorship or endorsement by the HWA on the anthology, the Chapter merely helped put it together).

Parts of this story are based in truth. My family and I were staying at a cabin down near Kanab, Utah, and it was situated in a similar setting and looked the same as described in this story. I took one of my daughters out exploring while my wife and other daughter stayed behind to get a nap. When I came back, she explained that she heard a crazy knocking noise coming from upstairs (which, by the way, contained a small door just like the story with a note saying do not open). We later found out it was a woodpecker and not the spirit of a deceased relative.

"The Temptation of the Moon to Shadow"

The forest holds secrets, old and dark
Some never meant to be discovered
Others, desperate in their desires
Calling out as loud as they dared
Searching for souls to come and play
Longing for lovers lost, and warriors brave
They found her one night, shining in the dark
A moon bright and bold against their shadowy intents
Just what they wanted, what they needed
Like a siren's song they sang to her
Soon, she found her way to the ancient tree
A towering creature, older than time itself
Swaying from its branches were hundreds of masks
Each one whispering mysteries and devilish delights
Come and join us, we've saved you a spot
Let your light ignite our shadowy desires
She listened to the words and wanted to play

Yet when she climbed the tree and put on a mask
Her light extinguished, and the shadows disappeared
She left the next day, disoriented and drained
The masked mourned her departure and cried out
Pleaded with her not to leave, promising dark things
If only she would stay with them a little longer
Their song was tempting, and so each month she returned
Staying for one night before leaving the masks behind
The forest holds secrets, old and dark
Some meant to be discovered

About the poem: I don't write much poetry. I have to be in a very specific mood and most of the time, I feel like I'm trying too hard. "The Temptation of the Moon to Shadow" came about when one of my friends posted a writing prompt on his blog involving a couple of those story dice. The dice depicted a tree on one and a mask on the other. I came up with the idea of a kid finding a tree full of masks. The tree tried to tempt the child closer. It evolved from there, for the better, I think. After I was finished, I saw an open call from the Horror Writers Association for their upcoming poetry showcase. I was quite amazed that I got picked up and featured among so many awesome poets. It was published by the HWA in their *HWA Poetry Showcase Vol 5* in September of 2018.

"The Cedar Box"

"E very noble elf of the Giltharu Empire who goes into the Hellwastes should be armed with a pistol and longsword, and they should never, either in camp or away, let those weapons leave their side. Between the varied tribal nations in the wastes, the great arch-wyrms, and the deadly sightless ones, the wastes are a land for the brave or foolish alone."

–Captain Brethwaite Vance, Yelwain's Cavalry

The noose tightened and bit into Zach's neck. He grunted as the rope burned and tore at his skin, and the pressure in his head grew. His hands were tied behind his back with a length of the same coarse rope. An elf wearing a faded green cavalry coat and a scar on his lip held the other end of the noose. He whipped it up and over a high tree branch then mounted his horse. He wrapped the rope around the horn of his saddle, clicked his tongue, and urged the horse forward. The rope tightened and pulled Zach up on his knees and then up to his tiptoes.

Zach focused on breathing. This wasn't the first time he had found himself in a noose. When he'd been captured for aiding the human tribes, a posse had strung him up and clipped his ears. It was a punishment worse than death for most elves, as they would never be able to return to the Giltharu Empire east of the Barrier Peaks.

Another elf, this one with a dead eye and greasy hair the color of coal, walked up to him. He pulled Zach's knife and gun from his belt and tossed them aside. Then, he pulled a small wooden box from his satchel.

The box itself was plain, cut from a cedar down near the Younger Wash. If Dead-Eye knew the care and time taken to make that box or the value of the contents inside, perhaps he wouldn't have thrown it from hand to hand so carelessly. Or perhaps he still would have because Dead-Eye didn't seem the type to place value on much, what with many of the elf's teeth missing and the remaining few stained blue with hocus dust.

"How do you open this, old timer?" Dead-Eye asked.

If they wanted what was inside, they'd have to figure it out themselves. Zach had traded several stag pelts to a shaman of the Magpie tribe to spiritually seal it. It would take knowing the command word to open it, or at least a decent hocus slinger to get that box open.

Dead-Eye scratched his scalp, pulled something from his hair, and examined it before flicking it away. "Don't make me rip the answer out of you."

Something rippled just under Dead-Eye's skin at the base of his neck. A small tremor of sorts, like a muscle twitch, but worse. There was something about the elf that stuck in Zach's craw, something unnatural.

The elf in the green coat stayed silent with head low. However, Dead-Eye's two other cronies stepped up beside him, yelling at the same time.

"Yeah, you best tell us or else, traitor!"

"Or else we'll gut ya and feed your clipped ears to buzzards!"

Dead-Eye held a hand up and the two buffoons quieted down.

"Last chance, old timer. We'll get this box open one way or another. If you tell us, we'll kill you quick, clean and such. Make us figure it out, and well..." Dead-Eye shrugged his shoulders and smiled. "...it won't be clean and such."

"You gonna stand there yappin' in my face all day?" Zach said through grit teeth. "If you plan on killin' me, do it. Otherwise, shut your mouth. Smells like an outhouse." It was difficult to talk with the noose around his neck, so it came out as more of a growl.

Dead-Eye nodded. "Very well, your way it is." He nodded toward the elf in the cavalry coat.

The elf urged the horse forward. Within moments, the rope pulled even tighter and lifted Zach off the ground. One of the other elves ran over and tied the rope off around a nearby tree, leaving Zach suspended.

Zach kicked and fought against his bonds as his lungs burned for air. The sky and tree branches blurred as his eyes teared up, bulging from the pressure of the noose. Dead-Eye stood before him with a stupid grin across his face, still holding the box.

"Just remember old timer, you brought this upon yourself."

With that Dead-Eye turned and mounted his horse, leaving Zach suspended from the tree. He didn't know how long it was before the darkness finally took him, but to Zach, it was forever.

Zach opened his eyes expecting to see the same desolate piece of landscape splayed out in front him. However, he found he wasn't outside. Timber walls of a log cabin enclosed him. Even stranger were the two red-haired, elven children that stared at him with wide eyes. They both wore wool, short-sleeved dresses. Patches of dirt and mud were on their face and clothes, and they wore no shoes. They were both the same height and age, and if Zach was correct, he guessed they were almost ten years old.

Zach tried to say hello, but his throat was raw, and it came out a raspy wheeze. The two girls ran out of the room. He lay there for a few moments and tried to muster the energy to get up. Everything hurt, especially his throat. The act of swallowing was like trying to swallow a prickle-plant without removing the spines.

A window allowed daylight to spill into the small room. The way the light danced in two different directions told him where the twin suns were in the sky. It was midday.

The room itself was barren of decoration. Only the bed, a rough-hewn chair with a bowl on top, and a nightstand with a small candle and tin cup accompanied him in the room. His belongings were nowhere to be seen.

Zach cursed under his breath and sat upright. The room spun, and he fell forward off the bed. Zach tried to catch himself but only managed to take the chair and bowl, which apparently held water, down with him to the floor.

"Delva's crooked finger, what are you doing?" a woman asked.

Zach tried to find the source of the voice, but every time he moved, the room spun a bit more. Calloused hands grabbed his arm and tried to lift him.

"Well come, I can't lift your sorry behind by myself. Quit being a sack of manure and help me out!"

Zach did the best he could, and with the help of the newcomer, he was back in the bed. Sweat beaded up on his forehead, and his chest heaved as he tried to get enough air. He hadn't been this weak since he almost died in the war. It was an unwelcome reminder of just how frail living creatures could become. However, it could have been worse. He could have been food for the buzzards. Zach had been lucky.

His mysterious benefactor was a tall female elf with hair that matched the children's color. It reminded Zach of that moment before the suns set just beyond the horizon and the sky lights up with brilliant reds and pinks. She wore a dirty white shirt, sleeves rolled up. Instead of a dress, she had on buckskin pants tucked into tall boots that had seen better days. Sweat poured down her face, washing tiny streams through the dirt on her cheeks.

"M'lady," Zach said and winced at the pain.

"Don't speak... It will take longer for you to heal. Now you nod yes or no to these questions, understand?"

Zach nodded.

"You're not some bushwhacker, are you?"

Zach closed his eyes and shook his head.

"Good. Cuz I don't need that kind of aura in this house. Second question. You got people looking for you?"

Zach didn't think Dead-Eye or his cavalcade of buffoons would come looking for him. They most likely thought he was dead. He shook his head again.

"Okay then. You don't mean me or my family any harm, do you? Cuz if so, you best just march right on out of here now. You won't like what I do if I find you steppin' to me or my children. You gonna behave?"

Zach nodded. She was not unlike the lions that lived in the great forests on the other side of the Barrier Peaks, gentle with their young yet could easily devour any elf fool enough to come between a mother and her cubs.

"Okay then. Now I'm not saying I just believed everything you said. However, I have a way of reading people and my gut says you may be okay. Plus, I found this in your belongings. Were you in the military?"

Sylvie held up a small silver medallion. Every soldier had been issued one upon enlistment. One side was engraved with a knot, the other was supposed to have his name. However, when he'd been captured and punished for helping the tribal nations, his captors had scratched his name away.

Zach nodded.

"My husband fought in those damn wars. Died there too, for all I know," Sylvie said and looked away. "Don't make me regret this decision, you hear?"

Zach nodded again as his mind started work overtime. Was this the family he had been searching for?

"My name is Sylvie. Sylvie Pine."

Perhaps he was luckier than he first thought. He *had* found them. Zach tried to sit up and say something, but the words caught in his throat. They came out as a garbled cry, and he fell limp in the bed.

"What did I just tell you? Don't speak! By the gods you're a sharp one, aren't you? Now you already met my girls. Get out here you two and introduce yourself proper to this man!" Sylvie said without turning.

There was a shuffle of feet, then the two girls reappeared at the doorway, still staring at him with those doe eyes.

"Girls, don't be rude."

They looked up to their mother then back to Zach.

"I'm Nym," said the first.

"I'm Pym," said the other.

Sylvie reached over and pulled them in front of her in a big hug. Both girls fought back against the embrace, but they had lost the battle before it ever began.

"Momma, is he a bad man?" Pym asked and pointed at Zach's head.

She probably meant his ears; the points had been cut off. Generally, he could hide it with a hat and bandana, but without either of those, his punishment was obvious.

"No, it don't mean he's a bad man. It just means he got in trouble with some folks who had a certain way of thinking," Sylvie said.

She tousled the girls' hair and then sent them out the door.

"Nymeranth and Pymethria. They're good girls, so don't mind them about what they said about your ears. We've helped our fair share of tribesmen in our time as well. Just never got caught," Sylvie said with a smile.

Zach held up his hands and shook his head, indicating he didn't mind at all.

"A little more curious than I'd like. It's gonna get them in trouble one day. However, it's cuz of their curiosity that you're alive, mister. See, they found you out there. Hell, your spirit had almost crossed the Great River."

Sylvie turned and walked out the door.

Zach sighed and stared at the ceiling.

Sylvie poked her head in again.

"Seriously though, don't make me regret this."

It was almost three days before Zach had enough strength to get up out of bed and walk around without help. His voice had started to return, although he couldn't speak much louder than a hoarse whisper without pain. There was so much he wanted to say, and he didn't have the voice to do so. Besides, without the box, what was the point? He was so close to delivering it, and now that chance had been snatched away by a gang of highwaymen who had caught him off guard.

He growled to himself and stood. His knees popped, and his body screamed at him to lay back down in bed, but the time for rest was over. Zach pulled on a red and black patterned shirt. It wasn't his, but it fit. At some point, Sylvie must have brought some of his things back because he found his hat, belt, and buckskin trousers next to the shirt.

Zach walked outside and shielded his eyes from the twin suns' shine. It was the first time he had been out since awakening in Sylvie's cabin. Sylvie stood by a small plot of corn, inspecting the stalks. The girls were running around chasing a chicken about the yard. Their giggles were infectious, and Zach almost cracked a smile. He had a family once—a wife, and two children. All of that had come to a sudden end. It was a period of his life he would have been more than happy to forget.

When the girls saw him, their faces lit up and they ran his way. Before he could do anything, they had grabbed his hands and were leading him toward a rickety chicken coop. The coop itself leaned to one side and was propped up with a few larger rocks stacked in a pile.

"You leave him alone, girls. He needs to rest," Sylvie said.

Zach shook his head. He'd been cooped up for far too long, and even though he knew he'd probably pay for it later, he needed to do something.

"Tools," Zach said.

The girls stopped and looked at him. Pym had her head cocked to the side and Nym scratched her scalp.

"Do you have tools?"

Zach flinched as the last word left his throat and everything burned.

Nym's eyes went wide, and an even wider smile appeared on her face. She nodded her head and ran off. Pym stayed behind and stared at Zach.

"Are you an outlaw? Cuz mamma don't like outlaws. She says they're no better than a damn Giltharu noble trying to lead a wagon train," Pym said.

"Pymethria Pine! You watch your language!" Sylvie said from nearby.

Pym took off after her sister.

Zach finished fixing up the coop just as the suns were finishing their descent. The moon was already high in the sky and visible and soon would wash the landscape in its bright light. It was a full moon, considered lucky by most Giltharu. However, to Zach, it just meant that it was easier to catch prey at night, and in the Hellwastes everyone was prey.

He was putting the tools back into the box when Sylvie and the girls came up behind him.

"I told you he was fixin' it, Mamma!" Nym said.

"I know, I know. I believed you both," Sylvie said. "You didn't have to do that, mister. We don't need your help."

Zach shrugged. Sylvie had been more than kind, and he wanted to help her and her family. He didn't know much about farming, but he was skilled enough to fix things. There were a few spots in the cabin that had caught his eye as well. He could get to those tomorrow.

Sylvie had horned hare stew ready when Zach entered the cabin. It was the season for horned hare, and Sylvie had shot a couple while he had been working. Both had been fighting as the clacks of their antlers bounced against the nearby canyon wall.

His stomach growled and he sat at the table. Pym and Nym had already eaten and sat near the fireplace reading an old book. Zach nodded toward them.

"Reading and writing are just as important as knowing how to hunt and work the land," Sylvie said. "We read each night before bed."

"Good," Zach said.

The stew was heavily seasoned with juniper berries and sage, and Zach's bowl was empty before it had a moment to cool. The warmth eased the pain in his throat, and the fullness in his stomach added to his exhaustion.

"Thank you. Night, m'lady."

"G'night, mister," Sylvie said.

The girls continued reading and Sylvie frowned. She let out a little cough to get their attention, but they were engrossed with their book.

"Girls, what do you say?"

They both looked up from the book and smiled.

"Goodnight!" they said in unison.

Zach gave them a traditional Giltharu farewell, touching his forehead with his first two fingers and then making a sweeping gesture to the side before following it up with a bow. Generally, it was followed with the phrase, "let the winds sweep you safely"; however, Zach was done speaking for the day.

He woke to the sound of screaming. It was the girls.

Zach rose from his bed, ready to rush out and see what was going on. However, a familiar voice made him stop—Dead-Eye.

"Miss Pine, I implore you to drop that scattergun before something just plain awful happens to these fine girls of yours!" Dead-Eye said.

Zach cracked open the door and peeked out. Sylvie stood in the doorway of the cabin with a shotgun in her hand. Outside the door stood Dead-Eye. He had an arm wrapped around Pym's neck and a knife in his other hand. The man in the green cavalry coat had Nym nearby. There were two others out there as well, mounted on horses.

"You let them girls go, or so help me—"

"So help you what, Miss Pine? I don't think you are in any situation to parlay with us. Now drop the gun," Dead-Eye said.

The back door of the cabin opened, and a short elf wearing a pair of scaled, arch-wyrmling chaps the color of sand crept in. The elf had a tomahawk made of knapped obsidian in one hand. Sheathed on the elf's belt was a long knife. Zach waited until the elf had passed by his door to make a move on him.

Zach opened the door as quietly as he could and snuck up behind him, striking like a canyon viper. Zach grabbed the elf from behind, covering his mouth and dragging him to the ground. Before the elf could strike, Zach rolled him over and drew the elf's knife. With a quick stab, he punctured the elf's lung. Chaps struggled for a few moments and Zach kept him quiet.

Sylvie looked back and her eyes went wide. Zach motioned her to stay quiet and turn her attention back to Dead-Eye.

Zach dragged the body into his room and took the elf's pistol and the obsidian tomahawk.

"How do I know you won't just kill us all if I drop this gun?"

"You have my word," Dead-Eye said.

"And I'm sure your word is worth its weight in hocus rock," Sylvie said.

Zach snuck out the back door and made his way to the corner of the cabin. He searched for any more of Dead-Eye's companions trying to make their way in but couldn't find any. That left the group out front, four total. Zach wished he had his gun.

Zach crouched low and made his way along the wall. He picked the shadowy side of the cabin and stuck to the darkest parts. Darkness was his world, and he could wear it like a buckskin coat when he wanted.

Two of the elves were still on horseback. One wore a wide-brimmed hat with a large peacock feather tucked into the hat brim. The other wore a long canvas duster. Dead-Eye and the green-coat still held Nym and Pym.

One of the elves was mounted on Ghost, a dapple grey with a white mane. Zach had found Ghost wandering the Hellwaste alone and nearly starved many years ago. Even half-dead the horse had a fighting spirit and had almost killed Zach with a well-placed kick. Damn fool didn't recognize help. It didn't take long for Ghost to warm up though. The sugar cubes and apples probably helped. They must have taken Ghost when they left Zach to hang. Zach's greatsword was still sheathed on Ghost's saddle.

Dead-Eye growled, and his eye flashed red. It happened so fast that Zach couldn't tell if had really happened at all or if it had been a trick of the moonlight. He remembered before when the elf's skin seemed to crawl. Zach tried to piece together what it all meant, but he didn't have time.

"I'm growin' tired of all this, Miss Pine! We offered you good money for this piece of land. You should have taken it. Now it's come down to this petty business. But I'm a reasonable elf, Miss Pine. You put down that gun, and we'll let you live and walk out of here," Dead-Eye said. "You have till the count of ten."

"I swear on Delva's crooked finger that you'll pay for this, both now and in the afterlife," Sylvie said.

The hairs on Zach's neck tingled as Sylvie said those words. Sylvie was throwing around some sort of witchcraft. It wasn't hocus. Hocus had a certain feel to it. The few times Zach had been around someone messing around with Hocus, it made his skin crawl and left a residue like bacon grease. The power behind her words was different—raw and savage like a thunderstorm.

Dead-Eye didn't seem to understand that he had just been cursed. Or if he did, he was about as smart as someone pokin' a stick at a sleeping gulch devil.

"Ten. Nine. Eight. Seven—"

"It's gonna be okay, girls. Trust me," Sylvie said.

Nym and Pym had wide eyes and tried to break away from their captors, but they didn't have the strength.

"Six. Five. Fo—"

Zach put two fingers in mouth and let out a shrill whistle that warbled through the air. Ghost let out a snort and bucked the elf off his back and trotted toward Zach. The distraction was enough for Nym to break away from the elf in the green coat. She ran towards Sylvie faster than a horned hare. Green coat drew his pistol and took aim at the girl's back, but Zach was already in motion. He ran toward them, and then when the distance felt right in his gut, he launched the obsidian tomahawk. The hawk buried deep into the elf's chest and the green coat looked down in surprise before he crumpled to the ground.

Ghost was close enough to Zach that the greatsword was in reach. Zach drew the weapon, its weight all too familiar in his hands. The other elf on horseback fumbled with his weapon. Fool. He should have had it out and ready long ago. It was a mistake the elf would never get to make again as Zach was upon him. Zach planted his feet in a wide stance and thrust with the sword, impaling the elf through the gut. The elf let out a pained cry and fell to the ground writhing. The horse ran off in fright, kicking up dust in the moonlight.

There was a rush of footsteps behind Zach, then a scattergun blast. Zach whipped around to find another one of Dead-Eye's elves, dead. Sylvie stood nearby, smoke wafting from one of the barrels of her gun. She winked at him then pointed the gun at Dead-Eye, who still held Pym. He wasn't smiling anymore.

Dead-Eye lifted Pym off the ground, using the girl to cover more of himself.

"Don't be hasty, Miss Pine. You shoot at me with that and you'll get us both now."

Zach started to flank him, but Dead-Eye turned his direction.

"And you! You should be dead already. One more step and I'll give this little lady a permanent smile."

Zach stopped his advance. Even if he had his pistol, there wasn't a clear shot.

"Now I'm going to ride out of here, and you're going to let me. Understand?" Dead-Eye said.

Sylvie took a step toward Pym, and Dead-Eye backed up.

"Nah, nah, you just stop. I'm taking the girl with me. When I get out of the pass, I'll let her go, you hear? Tell me you understand!"

Sylvie growled, and the ground beneath her trembled, small rocks around her dancing as the earth shivered. Zach caught her eye and shook his head. If she tried to cast something at Dead-Eye, she was likely to hit the girl.

Sylvie sighed and exhaled, and the ground stopped rumbling. "I understand."

Dead-Eye relaxed as well.

"Good."

Dead-Eye mounted his horse with Pym. The girl kicked and fought but couldn't get away from his grasp. He spurred his horse on and started to trot away.

Sylvie let out a cry and ran after Pym, but they soon were gone. Nym ran over to her mom and hugged her, sobbing.

"It's okay, we're going to get her back. Don't you worry. Are you okay?"

"Yes, momma."

Zach retrieved the obsidian tomahawk and cleaned the blade off on the elf's coat. Tucked in the elf's belt were Zach's black steel pistol and long knife. Zach spat on the ground and retrieved his weapons, putting them back in their proper place.

"You get your clothes on and take the trail to the Udlayin Homestead down by the creek. You remember how to get there?" Sylvie asked.

Zach didn't stay to listen to the rest. Ghost could catch up to Dead-Eye and Pym. He could save the girl, and he could hopefully retrieve his box if Dead-Eye still had it.

Dead-Eye had a head start, but Ghost was fast. It wasn't long before Dead-Eye's dust trail came into view. He was moving his horse with a purpose, but so was Zach.

Dead-Eye looked back, drew his pistol, and started firing. Bullets zipped by Zach's head, buzzing ferociously as they flew past his ear. Without warning, Dead-Eye turned his horse to follow a small game trail up the hill and nearly dropped Pym to the ground. She let out a shriek but clung to the horse. As fast as they were moving, falling from the horse could have been deadly, especially with all the rocks nearby.

Zach pulled on the reins and followed them. Dead-Eye was getting reckless and nearly drove his horse off the trail.

As they raced up the hill, a cave came into view, set into the mountainside. Dead-Eye pulled on the reins and stopped the horse. He jumped off and pulled Pym with him. Zach was right on his heels, sliding off Ghost's saddle.

He ran towards the cave when gunfire erupted from within. Zach dropped to the ground and rolled to cover behind a large boulder. Bullets hit the dirt where he just was, kicking up motes of dust.

Zach waited a moment. Pym's sobs grew more distant before almost disappearing. Zach made a mad dash for the next rock, but there weren't any more gunshots. He peeked out from around the boulder, but Dead-Eye nor the girl wasn't visible.

Zach moved towards the entrance of the cave but stopped as something caught his eye. Just above the cave's mouth was a large rock arch. He sniffed the air and caught it; the scent of death mixed with a metallic tinge. Zach had been around long enough to know the smell of an arch-wyrm.

"Come any closer, and the girl is dead!"

"Be smart about this," Zach yelled, although it wasn't very loud. Pain ripped through his throat with the action. "There's a posse coming for you!"

"That may be so, old timer! But that won't help you or this girl none!

"You don't want to hurt that girl; she doesn't have any play in this at all. Just let her go!"

"Don't think so. I let her go and I'm as good as dead!"

The damned fool didn't realize he was already as good as dead. All this yapping was going to wake that wyrm, and if Zach didn't get Pym out of there soon, she would be good as dead as well.

An idea came to him, one he didn't like but one that could work. He spat on the ground and holstered his pistol.

"Let's cut a deal, then," Zach said.

There was silence for a moment, and Zach wondered if they had gone further into the cave.

"What kind of a deal, old timer?"

"I take the girl's place."

"Not good enough! You think I'm stupid?"

Zach did, in fact, think Dead-Eye was stupid.

"Once you let her go, I'll give you the command word for the box."

The wind kicked up, blowing dust and tumbleweeds across the entrance to the cave. The clouds rolled past the moon and everything went dark as Zach waited.

"You throw your weapons down, you hear? You do that, then come on in!"

Zach stood, halfway expecting to get shot in the chest as soon as he did. However, Dead-Eye's pistol never barked. Zach drew his gun slow, making a big show of it, then threw it into the dirt.

"And that 'hawk you picked up! Don't play games with me, old timer! You want this girl to die?"

"Don't rush your rituals, I'm doing it," Zach said as he pulled the tomahawk from his belt. He let it drop to the ground and started towards the cave with his hands outstretched. "I'm coming in, don't shoot."

"Nice and slow, now! Nice and slow!"

Zach entered the cave. The tunnel was deep enough that the moonlight couldn't penetrate the darkness. It only took Zach a few moments for his vision to adjust. The dark shadows were replaced with a wash of light white and gray tones. The glow of Dead-Eye and Pym's eyes helped Zach pinpoint their location.

Dead-Eye and Pym stood behind a large outcropping of stone. Dead-Eye had his arm across her chest and pulled her tight against his body. He had his pistol pointed to the girl's head.

Tears streamed down Pym's face. She had a large bruise across her cheek that had swelled to the size of a goose egg.

"You okay?" Zach asked.

Pym nodded, but tears streaked through the dirt on her cheeks. Zach still had his knife, but Pym was too close for comfort. If he tried to throw the knife, he could easily hit the girl.

"Okay, I'm here, now let her go," Zach said.

Dead-Eye smiled and pointed the pistol at Zach.

"Give me the phrase to open that damned box!" Dead-Eye said.

Zach shook his head and took a couple of steps closer. "Let her go first, then I'll give you the words."

"What's in it? Gems? Gold?" Dead-Eye closed his eyes and took a deep breath. "Hocus?" Dead-Eye drew that word out as if just saying it gave him pleasure.

Pym bit Dead-Eye on the arm and stomped on the elf's foot at the same time. He let out a growl of pain and Pym broke free from the elf's grasp. Zach burst into motion, drawing his knife and letting it fly as Pym raced away from her captor. The blade flew past the girl and hit Dead-Eye just as the elf took a shot with his pistol.

The shot went wide, hitting the ground near Zach's foot and sending dirt flying into the air. Dead-Eye dropped to a knee and wrenched the knife out of his shoulder with a yell. Zach barreled into the elf and tackled him before he could get another shot off.

They rolled across the rocky earth, yet somehow Dead-Eye shifted the momentum and ended up on top of Zach. Dead-Eye let out a growl that sounded more animal than elf and head-butted Zach. The blow connected, and Zach's ears began to ring and his vision flashed.

Dead-Eye snarled and punched Zach in the face. A torrent of warm blood gushed from his nose and his eyes teared up. Out of instinct, Zach covered his head, but it exposed his mid-section. Dead-Eye wasted no time and dropped an elbow into Zach's chest and blasted the air from his lungs.

Zach tried to breathe, but he couldn't get any air in. He coughed and choked on blood that had run down his throat, filling his mouth with a coppery taste. Dead-Eye leaned in and grabbed Zach by the collar.

"You are going to die slow now, you hear me, old timer?"

Zach took a swing at Dead-Eye's jaw, but the elf blocked it and slapped Zach across the face. Zach could barely breathe and couldn't see more than blurred shapes. Dead-Eye's weight lifted from his chest as the elf stood and stepped back. Zach rolled to his stomach and crawled to where he hoped his knife was.

"I'll hire a blasted necromancer to raise your spirit from the dead, and I'll rip the command phrase from your soul!" Dead-Eye said. "But first, I'm going to take pleasure in making you bleed."

Zach's hand miraculously grazed the handle of his knife. He grasped it and rolled to his back, but Dead-Eye was already next to him. Zach stabbed with the knife. Dead-Eye dodged and knocked the blade from Zach's hand. Before Zach could do anything else, Dead-Eye had his pistol pointed at Zach's head.

Dead-Eye planted a boot in Zach's chest then aimed the pistol at Zach's leg.

"Where to start?"

"How about you shut your yap and just kill me already?" Zach said.

"Patience, old timer. I figured an elf like you would have learned patience by now. Some things take time." Dead-Eye pulled the hammer back on his pistol. "This will take time."

"You talk too much," Sylvie said, her voice coming from behind Dead-Eye.

Dead-Eye whirled around. Sylvie's scattergun roared, igniting the cavern with fire and thunder. The buckshot hit Dead-Eye square in the chest and the elf stumbled back as blood blossomed from the wound. He tripped over Zach's body and fell to the ground in a heap.

Zach's vision had started to return as Sylvie's face appeared before him. She frowned, looked over to Dead-Eye's body, and unloaded the other barrel into it.

"Come on then, let's get going," Sylvie said.

She helped Zach to his feet and every muscle in his body strained. His chest was tight, and he was fairly sure he had a cracked rib.

They shuffled toward the cave entrance, taking it slow and easy. Outside, Pym peered from behind a rock. When they got a bit closer, she came running forward and threw a big hug around Sylvie's leg. It almost knocked Zach over and he let out a grunt of pain.

"Sorry, mister," Pym said.

"It's okay. It's all okay now," Sylvie said. She stopped and faced Zach. "Thank you. Who knows what would have happened to my girl if you hadn't gone after him so quick."

Zach nodded. He moved forward but ran into Sylvie, who hadn't moved. He was about to say something, but the look of terror on her face followed by Pym's scream pulled his attention. Zach turned around and reached for his pistol. His holster was empty, and he remembered he hadn't recovered the weapon yet.

Dead-Eye got to one knee and let out a cough that was more bloody gurgle than anything. He stood and swayed from one side to the other and fell into the cavern wall. When he looked up at them, his good eye glowed red like burning ember.

"Gonna... kill..." Dead-Eye said with a voice full of death and grime.

"Pym, you get on my horse and go," Sylvie said as she reloaded the scattergun.

"No, Momma, I don't wan—"

"No arguing, girl, now go!"

Pym didn't say another word as she ran out of sight. Dead-Eye took a couple of shaky steps towards them with a drunken grin on his face. His chest was nothing more than a mess of meat and blood where Sylvie had shot him.

"Run," Zach said.

"Nope, don't think so," Sylvie said and emptied both barrels into Dead-Eye.

The scattergun hit him in the hip and leg and dropped him to the ground. Dead-Eye let out a croaking laugh. He propped himself up at the elbows and stared at them with his head cocked to the side. A stupid grin appeared on his face.

"Rip out... entrails..."

Smoke billowed from Dead-Eye's forehead as the skin blistered and bubbled. A jagged rune made of two diagonal lines encompassed within a diamond shape appeared as if branded on his skull. Zach knew the symbol. It was dark magic that not many knew, let alone practiced. It was demonic magic.

"Run. Your gun isn't going to kill him," Zach said.

"What is he?"

"He's a thrall."

Dead-Eye's laugh grew louder but turned to a scream as his bones popped and elongated, ripping through skin. His leg, destroyed by the scattergun, began to mend, but it sounded like snapping twigs as muscle and tendon realigned. The greasy hair on the elf's head grew thick and turned almost silver in color before covering his entire body.

"Sylvie, run!"

Zach walked backward and dragged Sylvie along. The motion must have broken through to her and she finally took his advice. She ran past him.

The pop and crack of bone stopped, and Dead-Eye stood. He had grown taller, almost as tall as the cave. He was covered in the silver fur and had sprouted a hairy tail that swayed back and forth like a big cat. The rune and his eye glowed blood red and pulsed rhythmically like a heartbeat.

Dead-Eye dropped to all fours and stalked toward Zach. Zach could run, but he didn't think he could get very far. He decided he'd stay, perhaps buy Sylvie some time to get away.

"Alright then, let's dance, you furry bastard!"

Dead-Eye let out a growl and crouched ready to pounce.

There came a rumble from back in the cave. Zach thought it was an earthquake at first, but the scrape of scale against stone told him otherwise. The arch-wyrm had woken.

Dead-Eye must have sensed it as well, as he spun around just as the wyrm came into view. It filled most of the tunnel, scales the color of sandstone. Two horns protruded from its skull into deadly points, while two more curled backward like a ram. It let out a roar and snatched Dead-Eye in its massive jaws, clamping down on his body with enough force that it vibrated Zach's chest.

Dead-Eye howled and clawed at the wyrm's face, but his claws did little to break through the creature's armored scales. The wyrm shook Dead-Eye's body from side to side. There was a massive crack as if a tree had fallen in the woods. Dead-Eye fell to the ground in two pieces. He let out a gurgled cry before the wyrm bit him again, this time on the head. The wyrm's jaw distended, and it began to pull Dead-Eye into his throat, much like a snake would devour its prey.

"Come on you damned fool!" Sylvie said.

Zach turned and found her mounted on Dead-Eye's horse. She had Ghost by the reigns. Zach ran as fast as he could, not wanting to find out if the wyrm was still hungry. His lungs burned, but he made it to Ghost. Ghost knelt down, allowing Zach to get onto the saddle with ease. Sylvie and Zach spurred their horses and galloped down the hillside back to the canyon path.

Pym waited at the bottom of the trail and started crying as they rode closer. Sylvie guided her horse close to Pym and embraced her in a long hug.

"It's okay. Let's go home," Sylvie said.

Zach checked the saddlebags on Ghost. He ensured his gear was there, secure and ready for the journey. Sylvie sat on a rocking chair outside of the cabin reading a book. Nym and Pym ran by laughing. Zach smiled. A part of him wanted to stay longer and help out with the myriad projects he'd found over the past week while properly healing. But another part of him needed to move on. The place and the family brought back too many memories. Memories he couldn't handle yet.

Before he could go, Zach had one last thing left to do. He dug the cedar box out of his saddlebag. When he found it stashed on Dead-Eye's horse, a wave of relief had washed over him.

When Sylvie saw what he held in his hands, her smile disappeared. She stood as he neared and put a hand on her chest.

"Is that what I think it is?"

"Yes," Zach said. His voice was starting to return, but it was still as jagged as broken slate.

Sylvie looked towards her girls. She opened her mouth as if she were going to say something but thought better of it. Her face tightened and she pursed her lips.

"It had been so long, I figured as much. Still, an elf could hope, right?"

Zach wanted to say something but couldn't find the words. Instead, he handed the box over to her.

She took the box with shaky hands and bit her lip. Tears began to well up in her eyes as she ran her fingers across the cedar.

"The command phrase is—"

"I know what the damned phrase is," Sylvie said.

She brought the box up to her lips and whispered the words, "*Elthwayne yeat dol arlhule.*" Ancient Giltharu for, "the moons chase the twin suns." It was a fancy way of saying our love is eternal.

Circular runes appeared, glowing a dark cerulean all across the box. Something internal clicked and the lid popped open.

Inside the box was a preserved elf heart wrapped in a buckskin pouch. It had taken Zach many days to process the hide and stitch it together. However, he knew his friend would have done the same.

"How... How did it happen?" Sylvie asked.

"We were ambushed by an orcish war tribe while scouting deep into the wastes looking for fresh water. My squad was pinned, and we fought long and hard against the orcs. He was wounded during the battle. Saved my life more than once, m'lady."

"Sounds like him. Always doing something stupid and brave."

Sylvie closed the box. The runes flashed blue again as the magic locked it.

"It was luck that you of all people found me," Zach said.

"Not luck at all. The winds have a way of blowing folk where they need to be. Thank you for this," Sylvie said.

Zach nodded and mounted Ghost. He tipped his hat to Sylvie. She nodded back, hugging the box to her chest. With that, Zach urged Ghost forward to allow the winds to take him where he was needed next.

About the story: I originally came up with this idea of a fantasy western back in 2015 after taking a vacation to Capitol Reef and Canyonlands. I love the scenery down there, and my mind raced with the possibilities. I thought it would be awesome to set a story in an Old West setting but with elves and such. I plotted this thing out for quite some time before actually writing it. Eventually, I'll turn this into a serial, as I already have the entire plot arc mapped out, but for now, I hope you enjoyed this opening tale. Also, this tale is connected to my *Dark Tyrant Series* and also my story, "The Devouring Maw." Let me know if you found the connection.

"Mr. Abernathy's Music Box"

I looked at the passenger manifest twice. Being a seafaring man, I had my share of superstition. While this didn't meet any known superstitions I could think of, the fact that Mr. Abernathy was listed as a passenger left a sick feeling in my stomach. That was enough to salt my drinking water.

To call Mr. Alistair Abernathy strange would be like calling President Lincoln tall—it was just fact. Everyone knew it, and everyone accepted his strangeness with a subconscious apathy. We ignored his odd mumbling and the way he shambled about town hunched over and constantly searching about. We even ignored his yearly tour around the town when he'd knock at each and every door asking the whereabouts of his wife.

She had died over ten years ago when their boat sunk near Sorrow Reef. A fisherman found him on the beach the next morning and said Mr. Abernathy just stood there staring out to sea with pieces of his boat washed up all about him. Story goes, Mr. Abernathy had nothing on his person but that music box he carries around tucked in his coat pocket. The authorities searched for his wife but couldn't find her. Bad business all around.

You could imagine my curiosity when I found Mr. Abernathy listed on the manifest. To my knowledge, the man hadn't left the Bay since he and his wife arrived from the Utah territories. Wasn't due to monetary concerns; supposedly he owned a mining outfit in Utah by the name of Angus. We assumed he stuck around after the accident because he waited for his wife. Yet, lest my eyes deceived me, his name sat atop of my manifest—Longboat Bay to London, England.

"Captain Bonnie, have you gotten a look at the manifest?" I asked.

The captain was a giant of a man. He always ducked when going through doors, and nobody ever looked down at him. With a large belly threatening every button on his shirt, and an ashen grey beard, Captain Bonnie was a formidable presence.

"That I have Mr. Grimes that I have. Is there something wrong?" he said.

"Everything's in order sir, with the exception of one passenger. Mr. Alistair Abernathy is booked to London, sir."

The captain raised an eyebrow and stroked his beard. Crumbs of bread fell to the wooden deck of the ship.

"And the problem is what, Mr. Grimes?"

I found myself having trouble trying to formulate a proper response to his question. What was the problem?

"Do you think it wise to let someone in his state on board, sir?"

"And what state would that be?"

"His mental state, sir."

The captain let out a sigh that could have filled the mainsail. He took the passenger manifest from me, folded it up, and stuffed it in my coat pocket.

"Mr. Grimes, the poor Mr. Abernathy paid in full for this voyage. He paid extra, in fact. Enough to convince me to alter our course slightly."

I opened my mouth to protest, but the captain held a finger up and stopped me before I could utter a word.

"The alteration won't delay us any, Mr. Grimes. Now I suggest you let him be and get back to ensuring we are ready to go. Do I make myself clear?"

The steely glint in the captain's eye was enough to tell me to drop the matter. He wouldn't budge, and it wouldn't do to argue further in front of the crew. It was bad enough that we'd have to make the voyage with Mr. Abernathy.

"Clear as mermaid's tears, sir."

"Good. Now make ready. The winds are in our favor."

As we made preparations to depart, the passengers boarded. We didn't have many this time, and I could understand the captain's willingness to allow anyone aboard if they had the money to pay. Yet, as Mr. Abernathy stepped onto the deck, Death used my spine as a concertina. Mr. Abernathy slunk on board, looking all about as a criminal would. He'd bring nothing but bad luck on the voyage. I would have to keep a watchful eye on him.

Mr. Abernathy slipped beneath deck to his quarters and remained unseen for the rest of the day. We pushed off from the bay and made our way to open water. It was good to be out at sea again. The rise and fall with the waves, the salty spray in the air, it was heaven.

"Have you seen her, my wife?"

I spun around to find Mr. Abernathy behind me. He clutched the wooden music box in his hands, his knuckles white with exertion.

"Mr. Abernathy, your wife is dead. You know this. Please stay out of the crew's way. The deck is very dangerous."

I tried my best to keep my wits about me, but being so close to the man put me on edge. My hands shook, and I couldn't help but stare into Mr. Abernathy's dead eyes. I would be happy when we pulled into London and offloaded him. We'd all be better off.

"Not dead. Just waiting."

He fiddled with the music box and twisted the crank. The old gears whizzed and sputtered, but no music came out. Yet that fact didn't stop Mr. Abernathy from swaying to and fro to a tune which apparently only he could hear.

"Waiting for what?" I asked.

He stopped swaying to the imagined tune and stared me directly in the eyes.

"Waiting for me."

With that, he scurried off below deck with the music box to his ear. The winds picked up and licked at the sails. The sun dipped low beyond the horizon and cast the sky in a sanguineous glow. Following the luck with Mr. Abernathy, the red sky didn't bode well. We were in for a bumpy ride.

My prediction blossomed to life at twilight. Dark clouds rolled over us and brought with them all the moaning and groaning Poseidon could muster. The waves tried to drag us under, but the *Scarlet Whale* was a stubborn bitch. It'd take more than a squall to send us to the deep.

The heavy footfalls of the captain vibrated behind me. The big man looked to the storm and then to me.

"Mr. Grimes, make sure all the passengers are safely secured down below. We wouldn't want anyone taking a midnight swim."

"Sir!"

I accounted for everyone with the exception of one passenger—Mr. Abernathy. Thunder boomed above deck, and the sea decided it was a good moment to throw the ship. I had good sea legs but still fell. My head hit the wall, and for a moment, I couldn't see straight. The rush of waves and the creak of the ship sang to me, but something else floated to my ears, a melody of some sort. The sound came as fast as it went, but I couldn't shake the song from my head.

Lightning cut across the dark skies and left a squall of light floating in my vision. The same music crawled into my ears again, and just as I thought I recognized the tune, thunder bellowed and drowned the notes away. I grabbed the railing and heaved up to my feet.

The *Scarlet Whale* rode the waves as if they were made of broken glass—beautiful and sharp, yet deadly if handled wrong. Captain Bonnie had more experience on the sea than most people I had ever met; therefore, I wasn't worried about the ship. I was, however, worried about the safety and well-being of the people on board the ship, even Mr. Abernathy. Whether I cared for the man or not didn't matter. I was in charge of his safety, and I intended to keep him safe.

I found Mr. Abernathy at the bow. He stood at the very edge of the deck, and if it weren't for the railing, I had the feeling he would have walked right into the dark waters below. A tall fellow by the name of Jacob stared at Mr. Abernathy. Jacob had a thick island accent which many couldn't understand, but he did his work and could lift more than anyone else I had ever seen. He simply stood and wrung a red cap in his large hands, over and over again.

I walked behind him and placed a hand on his shoulder. Jacob started at my touch and whirled around to face me. His eyes were wide, and the whites were clearly visible, which created a strange contrast the man's mahogany skin.

"Go check on the cargo, if you would. It would be our end should it come unsecured during this swell," I said.

Jacob didn't say anything, just nodded. He made his way below deck, but not before casting another glance toward Mr. Abernathy. I motioned him below deck. He nodded and disappeared.

The sea shook us and caused the ship to list to the side. I grabbed onto the rail again to keep from falling overboard. Somehow, Mr. Abernathy stayed onboard during all this. The man clutched the music box tight to his body and stood motionless. He was on the lookout for something.

"Mr. Abernathy! We must get below deck!"

If he heard me, he didn't show it. I inched closer to the man. The waves came at us harder and faster, which made any movement difficult. The ship swam with the sea, but walking was almost impossible—up and down, side to side. Even Captain Bonnie would have a hard time moving through this.

"Mr. Abernathy! Please, I implore you we mu—"

The music cut me off. It came clear as if I sat center theater next to an orchestra. A soft melody that rode the wind as we rode the waves. The music seemed to overpower the thunder and the storm's bluster. Soon, the only noise in my head was the sound of my own breathing and the music.

Mr. Abernathy lifted the music box over his head. He closed his eyes and smiled. The *Scarlet Whale* listed with a violence that took me off my feet. I slammed onto the deck, and for a moment, only a high-pitched ringing filled my ears. Then the damnable music washed up in my consciousness again.

Saltwater came aboard once more and slammed me against the smooth wood. This time, instead of knocking the sense from me, it gave me focus and pulled me back to reality.

Mr. Abernathy's cackle of joy cracked into the night air. I struggled to get my feet under me while the ship fought the sea. Finally, I stood.

Mr. Abernathy dropped the music box at his feet. The man stared out into the inky darkness.

"We need to get below deck!" I said.

He didn't say anything but continued to search. Perhaps if I could get the music box, the man would listen. It would be the last attempt before I left him to Poseidon's will.

I used the rail to get close. Even with its support, movement was very difficult. The ship tried several times to throw me into the drink. A sense of duty kept me moving even though I wanted to turn around and head to the safety of the hold. Let the Sea take Mr. Abernathy and his lunacy. I almost turned around right then, but I was so close. The wooden box was nearly within arm's reach. With one hand clamped onto the rail, I extended my other arm out. The tips of my fingers brushed across the intricate carvings of the music box, then the ship lurched, and the box rolled away.

I cursed and crawled toward the box. I knew if I tried to walk, I'd only risk more injury. The box sat on its side with the lid open. The music still played in my head, but not from the contraption only an arm's length away. It came from the sky. It played from the sea. The waves and wind worked in concert to produce a haunting melody which saturated the very core of my being. I knew if I survived this storm, I would never hear another song so lovely and haunting. The box was just within reach. I stretched out to grab it, confident it would help lure Mr. Abernathy below deck.

Mr. Abernathy grabbed my arm, his hand clamped down on my wrist like a crab claw. A smile was perched upon his face, but his eyes were distant.

"My wife, Mr. Grimes. I know you'll like her. She's such a lovely lady and always enjoyed company."

I tried to wrest my arm away, but something caught my eye. It was just a glimpse of a shadow in the darkness, silhouetted in a flash of lightning. A crag of sharp rock loomed in front of the ship and stretched high into the air telling me where we were—Sorrow Reef.

Mr. Abernathy sunk to his knees and whispered into my ear.

"I found her."

Just before we hit the reef, I saw her in the waters, ghostly and pale with a grin on her dead face that would have turned Blackbeard's blood cold.

About the story: I wrote this tale back in 2013. I can't quite remember too much about the backstory, but I believe I came across a piece of art that inspired me. I posted this on my website in 2014 as a freebie for hitting 100 likes on Facebook. If you go on my website you can still find it; however, the ending is slightly different than this version. I felt like this version had a bigger impact.

"The Horror of Sunshine Meadows"

I wish I could forget what happened that day in the woods. Whenever I think on it too long, my eye spasms and a phantom pain shoots through the space where two of my fingers used to be.

It occurred twenty years ago. School had ended early that day, and I was excited to get home. The route to my house skirted along a large expanse of woodland curiously named Sunshine Meadows. Curious, because the trees were so thick the sun's heavy rays were unable to smash through the forest's rampart of green pines.

The dark character of the woods had burrowed its way into the imagination of the town's population. Parents told ghost stories to their children about the woods in hopes that they'd stay away. The quality of the forest, doubled with the dreadful tales, created a very real atmosphere of apprehension for most people. I, being young and rebellious, gave the warnings no heed.

I trekked home, oblivious to my surroundings, at least until something standing at the tree line made me stop in my tracks—a young girl wearing a pink dress, clutching a yellow balloon.

The girl waved, turned around, and walked into the black expanse of trees. With two steps, the tall pines had swallowed her. Her yellow balloon drifted upward until it caught on a tree branch. It wriggled to break free, but the woods wouldn't let it go.

The forest was no place for that little girl. Even at my young age I knew that much. I ran after her and yelled for her to come back. Her pink dress stood out amongst the trees, and I was able to find her. Within moments I was almost upon her. At the last moment, she stopped and turned away from me.

She started to giggle, and my steps faltered. It wasn't the normal, infectious laugh of a child. It was different, lower in tone and filled with gravel. My body screamed at me to leave, turn tail, and run all the way home and swear to any higher power that would listen to me that I'd stay away from these cursed woods. However, against all the warnings, I put a hand on the girl's shoulder.

The giggles turned into demoniacal laughter. That was when she spun around.

I can't recall the details of her face. It's blurred in my memory, and I'm thankful for that. However, her teeth... By god, her teeth remain etched in my mind. Sharp and plentiful. More teeth than any human should possess.

My parents found me in my room later clutching my bleeding hand. They said I kept muttering incoherently in the corner.

My medications make me drowsy. Most days I'd take comfort in watching the world from my window as sleep takes me. However, today, caught in the limb outside my window, is a floating yellow balloon.

About the story: "The Horror of Sunshine Meadows" was a fun piece of flash fiction I wrote for Books of the Dead Press. They picked it up and featured it online back in 2013. It was my sixth published piece of work. It was a great experience, but it was shortly after this that I decided I wasn't going to write for free anymore. I have since cleaned this up and featured it on my Curious Fictions profile. If you want to read more things like this, check it out.

"Final Moment"

To call the painting disturbing was the understatement of the century. Harriett fought the urge to step away. Instead, she forced herself to soak in all the particulars of the horrifying piece of art. The fine details captured on the child's face were almost too real. What could frighten a boy so terribly?

It was an oil painting of a small boy and his dog. The boy wore a shirt and trousers made of a plain cloth that was the color of moist earth. Why moist earth popped into her head, she couldn't say. Moist earth... clay... dirt freshly dug up from the cemetery.

Harriett closed her eyes and took a deep breath before looking once more at the painting.

The boy clutched a book in one hand as if it were some grand treasure. The artist had even taken care to paint the whites of the boy's knuckles. In the boy's other hand was a leash leading to a black and tan English Foxhound.

In the background, there was a wooden cabin. A shadowy figure stood in the window with dull candlelight glowing behind it. Smoke billowed from a chimney and filled the dusky sky, mixing with dark rain clouds.

Yet, none of those details concerned her more than the fear on the child's face. The boy was taking a step back, his blue eyes splayed wide in terror. The dog at his side raised its hackles, its mouth pulled back in a menacing sneer.

It raised a Jeopardy board of questions in Harriett's mind. What Scares Little Boys in the Creepy Painting for 100, Alex.

She hugged her chest and wished she had brought her coat in from the car, but it was too late now. The auction would start soon.

Harriett took one last look at the painting and decided right then and there that she wanted it. She marked down the auction number as well as the painting's title: *Final Moment* by Anonymous—1716.

The auction house was a hive of activity that grated on her nerves, making it difficult to focus on what anyone was saying. The harder she tried, the louder the buzzing became. The cacophony grew and grew until her lunch almost crawled out of her stomach and onto the floor.

Dizziness rolled through her and threatened to take her to the ground when a large man, who was almost spherical, grabbed her shoulder. As soon as he touched her, the incessant buzzing stopped, and the nausea all but disappeared.

"You okay?" The man's voice was deep and full of concern.

Harriett nodded and squeaked out her thanks before ambling away. She debated whether or not she still needed to hit the restroom when the speakers flared to life and feedback from the auctioneer's microphone screeched into existence.

The auctioneer tapped the mic a few times before he tugged at his black tie. After another moment to ensure he had everyone's attention, he leaned forward.

"I would like to welcome everyone to our fifth annual auction here at the Canyon Shadows Museum of Art and History. We have a lot of lovely pieces today, all of which I hope to find new homes for. Without any further delay, let us begin."

The crowd started clapping like an army of automatons, moving in sync as if someone lit one of those "applause" signs. Harriett looked about and finally decided to take a seat. The thought of missing out on the *Final Moment* was too intense. The desire to own the painting dominated her very being.

It was strange. She found the painting horrifying on a primal level, yet there was a part of her deep down inside her bloody viscera that yearned for it. Harriett couldn't explain the feeling.

After forty-five minutes of waiting through other paintings and sculptures, her piece finally arrived on the pedestal. There it sat under heavily lit florescent lighting which glazed the picture with its alien glow.

"You'll notice that this piece shows a realistic depiction of a young Puritan boy and his dog. The artist is unknown, but the date on the title is correct. This piece came from the New England Colonial Art Gallery at Miskatonic University. We'll start the bidding at 500 dollars. Do I have 500 dollars?"

As soon as the auctioneer threw a number out, he slipped into the sing-song rhythm typical of his trade. Harriett raised her paddle and the auctioneer pointed at her.

"I have 500, can I get 600? 600 dollars? 600 dollars! Do I have 700?"

Harriett raised her paddle again and searched the crowd as the auctioneer barked out her bid. She wanted to see who was competing against her. After a moment, she spotted him. The sphere of a man who had helped her earlier raised his own paddle and caught her eye. He nodded a gentleman's nod, almost a salute stating he was ready for the duel.

She returned the gesture and turned back to the auctioneer. She rose the paddle and called out, "1000!"

The crowd of people gathered at the small auction house turned in their seat to see who had raised the stakes. Harriett watched her opponent's face redden, and his eyes squinted almost shut.

"1000 dollars, do I have 1100? 1100 dollars? 1000 dollars going once!"

"1100," the fat man stated, pulling a handkerchief from his pocket. He used the flimsy cloth to dab at his sweat-ridden brow.

Harriett turned her attention from the man and looked back at the picture. She needed to help the boy, to find out what was happening to him and why he shrank away from whatever was in front of him. She desperately wanted to know why the boy was trying with both hands to keep the dog from getting away.

Both hands? Where was the book? He had a book before. She scanned the painting looking for the worn-out book and found it at the boy's feet.

"1100 going twice!" the auctioneer called, pulling her focus back to the present.

"2000!" Harriett yelled, raising her paddle high.

The fat man threw his paddle down and turned away from her. She had won.

"2000 dollars going once! 2000 dollars going twice!"

The auctioneer paused dramatically and scanned the crowd.

"Sold to number 81612! Please head to the front desk to make your payment and collect your lovely work of art."

Harriett rushed to the payment kiosk. After transferring the funds around in her accounts, she was out the door with the painting in tow.

When she got home, she pulled the packaging off the picture and looked upon it again. The book was back in the boy's hand. Everything was back in its proper place.

It must have been nausea or dizziness. Or perhaps she was caught up in the moment of the auction and hadn't seen things properly. It didn't matter, the painting was back to normal.

She leaned it against the wall and went searching for something to mount it. Perhaps if she hadn't been in such a rush, she would have noticed that the silhouette in the window of the cabin was no longer there.

That night, a scratching at her bedroom door woke her from a fitful sleep. She sat up trying to figure out what the noise was or where it was coming from. It sounded like a dog scratching, snarling, and whining as it tried desperately to get in. Harriett flipped the light on by her bedside and padded closer to the door. The scratching stopped, effectively stopping her in her tracks as well.

She leaned closer to the door but heard nothing. Harriett went to the dresser drawer and opened it. Moving some of her undershirts out of the way, she reached down and tapped the key code into her small gun safe. It clicked open with a soft *click* and she grabbed her pistol. The gun was a gift from her ex-husband back when they were still married. He had been afraid that while he was away on business someone would break in and she would be defenseless. For the first time in a long time, Harriett was pleased with one of her ex-husband's decisions.

She slammed a magazine into the gun and racked the slide back. Harriett went to the shooting range at least once a month, and the actions came smooth and natural to her.

She took a deep breath and then threw the door open, pointing the gun out in front of her. Deep scratches scarred the wooden floor in front of her bedroom. She took her time moving down the hall, scanning each room as she passed by.

Something crashed in the living room, and her heart skipped a beat.

The flood of adrenaline added to her already shaken nerves, and she had to actively concentrate to keep the gun steady. She rounded the corner to the living room, the pistol ready to take down any would-be attackers.

The lamp lay on its side near the sofa, still rocking slightly from falling over. Putting one foot in front of the other in controlled steps, she made her way to the edge of the sofa. A soft growl met her ears, and something rustled around with the lamp.

It was a dog!

"Get out of here!"

The growling got louder and rougher, more akin to something feral than a domestic breed. She took two deep breaths and stepped around the sofa ready to put the creature down.

Nothing was there.

The growling faded away. She circled the couch looking everywhere. She even dropped to all fours and looked under the furniture. Nothing. Harriett let out a sigh and righted the lamp, and when she turned to check the rest of the house, she almost ran into the small boy from the painting.

Harriett let out a shriek and sat up. She was back in her bed.

Her heart was pounding, and she was covered in sweat. Harriet raced out of the bedroom, springing across the floor like a gazelle. There were no scratches on the door. She ran into the living room only to find it in order as if nothing had touched it.

Harriett turned to look at the picture. What she saw froze her blood.

The dog was missing from the painting.

The dog wasn't the only thing that had changed. The boy's expression had turned from fear to cruel wickedness tinged with a sour, mischievous grin that threatened to jump from his face.

It was a smile that reminded Harriett of Justin McCoy. Justin had been Harriett's classmate in 1st Grade. One day after recess, the class came back to find Justin squeezing the class's pet hamster Booger. Booger was obviously dead, and Justin was simply grinning at everyone as if he had just won a gold star for excellence.

She grabbed the painting and ripped it from the wall. The hardware didn't let go of the nail, and she ended up pulling out a large chunk of the drywall along with the picture.

Harriett let out a scream of frustration.

She made a promise with herself to patch the hole in the morning. Cursing under her breath, she marched the painting out to the nearby dumpster. The dull thud that echoed as it hit the bottom of the steel container gave her a sense of satisfaction, and she returned to bed.

Morning came too soon. The sunlight blasted through her cheap blinds and pounded at her eyes. She finally gave in to the insistent raging of the light and got out of bed. Harriett fell into her routine with ease and set about her morning ritual: take a shower, brush the teeth, and listen to National Public Radio while picking out what to wear. The comfort of her routine was shattered when she left the bedroom.

She was headed down the hall to the living room and happened to steal a glance back toward the bedroom only to find the painting hanging off the back of her bedroom door. Harriett spun around and tripped over her own feet, falling onto the floor.

She crawled toward the picture and found it was devoid of the boy and the dog. The windows in the cabin were dark and empty as well.

She tore the painting down and threw it against the floor. It hit the ground face up mocking her efforts. Her heart heaved in her chest when the *click-clack* of toenails hitting the linoleum rang out from her kitchen, followed by a low growl rumbling in the living room.

Harriett grabbed the nickel-plated doorknob to her bedroom and gave it a twist. It started to turn but caught on something, refusing to turn. She continued to try and force the knob around, but it was as if something had a hold of it from the other side. In a last-ditch effort, she grabbed the knob with both hands and turned with every ounce of strength she could muster. It wouldn't budge.

A muffled giggle from a small child slithered into her ears from behind the door.

She scrambled backward a couple of steps. The knob turned, and the door slowly opened.

There was a pitter-patter of little feet running around her bedroom. She instinctively reached for the door to investigate; however, something stayed her hand. Her fingers hovered over the knob, shaking slightly.

Harriett decided not to and pulled her hand away. The bedroom door slammed shut with so much force it shook the foundation of her home, causing her to jump and take a few more steps back. Pain flashed in her foot, causing a scream to escape her lips. She fell to the floor, banging her elbow and head on the way down.

Stuck in her right foot was the nail that had been holding the painting up.

Harriett touched the bloody nail and let out another gasp as agony shot up her leg. Tears started to brim at her eyes. She gritted her teeth and grabbed onto the nail and slowly pulled it from her foot. As it cleared skin, she let out a deep breath and flung the nail down the hallway. Some of the blood landed on the painting. The blood disappeared as if the painting itself had drunk it up.

One moment the flecks of blood were there, the next, gone. She looked at the picture and tried to see if it had stained, but no trace of the blood was on the old canvas. However, the light in the window of the cabin was on again, and the tall shadow was visible.

The dog barked from the living room startling Harriett. From the sound of it, she figured it was standing at the end of the hallway. She didn't want to look. She couldn't. Something told her not to turn her head or it would be the last thing she ever did. Harriett brought her knees to her chest and clutched them close to her body.

The door to her bedroom clicked open again. This time, it was dark in her room. She couldn't see the sunlight that should have been there. She couldn't hear NPR from the bathroom anymore. It was quiet and dark.

The door opened further, and a light appeared, yet it wasn't sunlight. The light was a low glow of a candle that flickered as if alive, sending shadows dancing and cavorting about in macabre merriment. From the corner of the room rose the silhouette of a tall lanky individual.

The *click-clack, click-clack* came from behind her followed by a dog's huffing. A small pale hand appeared from behind the door accompanied by a child's giggle. Harriett closed her eyes tight and tried to wake up.

Yet this wasn't a nightmare. She wasn't sleeping. Harriett tried to crawl away, but two hands—small hands, but freezing cold—grabbed her by the ankles. Whoever had her yanked her into the bedroom.

The door slammed shut and darkness consumed her. She couldn't see anything, but she wasn't alone. There was the soft panting of a dog and a low giggle of a child.

About the story: "Final Moment" has gone through a lot of rewrites and revisions. It's one of those stories that never felt good enough or finished. I liked the concept well enough. I originally wrote it for a residency workshop at Seton Hill for my MFA. It was well received. After the final rewrite, I think it's ready. :)

"The Demons We Bring"

Utah Territories, 1866

The rain poured down as if God just didn't care anymore. Hell, maybe He didn't. My clothes were soaked through, and the chill crept into my spine. Nothing a shot of whiskey wouldn't cure.

The thunder bellowed from above, rumbling through the mountains. The roar drowned the man's whimpers of pain as he crawled away from me.

I pulled the hammer back on my Peacemaker and put my boot across his back. With a slight push, I knocked him to his belly. Blood pooled from the wound in his side, only to be picked up and washed away in a ruddy tributary.

"Please, don't kill me," the man said.

Some nerve he had to beg me, of all people.

I crouched down. Far enough away that he couldn't try anything funny but close enough to see the whites of his eyes.

I dug deep into my coat pocket until the sharp edges of the daguerreotype bit my finger. The picture was usually comforting, but this time its weight tugged on my soul. I pulled it out and let the soft glow of the cloud-covered sun wash over the small memento. Raindrops collected on the metal picture, and I had to wipe the moisture away to reveal my wife and son. Everyone called my wife Sally because they couldn't pronounce her native name. I think she liked it. She had the most beautiful black hair and a set of brown eyes richer than chocolate from the general store.

Then there was Samuel, my handsome boy. I think he was amazed at the equipment and somehow sat still long enough to let the man capture his image. When I showed him the daguerreotype, he just giggled and clapped his hands. They were my family, they were everything, and because of this sonofabitch, they were gone.

I slid the picture back into my pocket then pointed the gun at the man. He rolled to his back and put his hands up.

"Mister, plea—!"

The blast from my pistol drowned the rest of his words away in a mix of blood and smoke.

Name's Jeremiah Abraham Redford, and I've been living in Hell for over a year now. Those bastards killed my family because they were different. Dragged them out of my house and hanged them in our oak tree. Samuel loved that tree. The lawmen didn't care much, and never did anything to punish those responsible. Well, I just killed the last one of those cowards.

The rain continued to pour from the sky. It was cold, miserable, and just didn't do a damn thing to improve my mood. I should have felt better sending the coward to meet his maker, but I was empty. The medicine man from Sally's tribe said I wouldn't get anything out of killing her murderers. He mentioned it would only leave me open to the bad spirits, and my actions would take me to a darker place. I was already in a dark place. At least now, I didn't have to share that place with her murderers.

My fingers found their way into my pocket and brushed the thin metal. Sam's laughter danced through the pines, or was it just the wind? For a moment, the wind on my face was replaced with Sally's soft touch, with a gentle caress behind my ear.

The trail started to wash away under the torrent, but I was able to pick a path down the mountain. Pines and aspens swayed in the storm and would have put me to sleep if it weren't for the rain.

A child's whimpering skipped along the wind. It was probably just my mind playing tricks again, so I ignored it. What I couldn't ignore was the smell of bacon in the pan. No man worth his salt could ignore such a delicious smell, especially in this hellish cold.

Smoke from a campfire floated up into the evening air. I turned toward the smell and ambled closer. My hand rested on the butt of my pistol. Who knew what I would find in these woods.

"Well, mister, you best come on out," an older man said with a voice full of spit and gravel.

Something about the way the man spoke raised my hackles. I didn't like him, but I didn't like being cold and wet, and he did have a cook-fire blazing.

I urged my horse around the big pine and the campsite came into view. The man sat on a log with his back to me. He wore a dull grey capote, common attire for mountain men, with the hood pulled up over his head. I was about to speak when something large fell to the ground in a wet spatter.

A dead elk dangled from a frayed rope attached to a tree. Its insides had fallen into a large pile just below the carcass. The wind shifted and the smell of the animal hit me and made me want to retch. Given the state of the elk's body, it had been hanging for some time.

The cook fire gave off a hellish light and revealed a small wagon full of dead animals in various states of rot. The rain slowed and flies started buzzing around the cart in a cloud of annoying movement.

"Well, are you going to come closer or just stand there lookin' stupid?" the man asked.

The steel edge in the man's words and the way he cocked his head tickled my spine and made me want to turn my horse around. But it was getting late, and I needed to get out of the cold. With my clothes wetter than a shot glass on Saturday, I wouldn't last long in the chill.

I eyed the animals as if they would spring to life at any moment. Could have been a trick of the firelight, but I swore they moved every so often. I hitched my horse to a pine and moved closer. The heat's embrace was nice against my cold hands, and I took a moment to rub the feeling back into my fingers. Before I sat down on a log opposite to the stranger, I opened my coat and made a point to flash my gun—I didn't want any trouble and hoped the stranger didn't want any neither.

"Didn't catch your name," I said.

The hood covered the man's face, and I couldn't make out any features other than a long, tangled beard with the same bloody hue as southern Utah clay.

"I didn't throw it," the man said. "But you can call me Obadiah."

A common enough name, but when he spoke it out loud, a wave of sickness rolled through my gut, and I almost lost what little food was left in my belly. There was power in the man's words, and it wasn't good. My mind told me to get the hell out of there, but I wasn't known for running. Not from anything.

"I'll just warm myself, dry my clothes, and be on my way," I said.

Something shifted in the wagon of dead animals. I spun and drew my pistol in the span of a breath, but there wasn't anything there.

Obadiah let out of a wet laugh that clung to the air. The laughter slithered into my eardrums like worms through a corpse.

"A bit jumpy, aren't you, Jeremiah?"

I kept the gun out and readied as I turned toward the old man. Cold or not, it wasn't smart staying here.

"I never told you my name, old timer."

Again, Obadiah let out a laugh which echoed through the woods. A child whimpered again in the darkness, closer this time.

"The woods told me who you are—and what you're after."

Obadiah was cracked. I pointed the gun straight at the old man's chest.

"You best start making some sense, old timer. Did one of Theroux's men send you?"

I put a bullet through Theroux's skull less than an hour ago—sent that sonofabitch to meet Old Scratch himself—but that didn't mean the bastard didn't bring others to protect his worthless hide.

Obadiah reached up and pulled the hood of his capote away with twisted, arthritic fingers. The firelight fell across the old man's face and revealed a bald head full of liver spots and wrinkles. Heavy bags sank beneath the man's eyes and gave him a tired expression. While he didn't laugh anymore, there was a hint of a grin in the corners of his mouth and a crazed spark behind his eyes. Obadiah lacked many of his teeth, but the few he retained were sharp and jagged.

"They sent me to help you."

"Help me what?" I asked.

"Get your family back."

My breath caught in my throat as I forgot how to breathe. Then the child's cry twisted in the wind again, and I couldn't help but flinch and gasp for air. The cry was low and full of pain and took me back to a night I never wanted to remember.

"Sam?" I spoke to no one in particular—my voice barely a whisper.

"I'm afraid not, Jeremiah. But I know who can bring your boy back."

Obadiah's lips curled into a smile, larger than any smile I'd ever seen. The old man's coat rippled and moved in places it shouldn't have moved.

I sneered, then spat into the dirt. My blood boiled and helped chase the cold from my bones.

"I've had about enough of this nonsense. You've got five seconds to spit out something useful or you're going to be as cold as a wagon wheel!"

His coat moved again, and I caught a glimpse of a furred tail from one of his sleeves.

"If you could get your family back, what would you be willing to do, Jeremiah?"

I was raised by my Pa to be a God-fearing Christian; however, something broke inside me when I found my Sally strung up by her neck. I'd sell my soul to the devil if I could get my family back.

Obadiah's smile somehow grew larger, and I almost shot him on principal. He chuckled and leaned forward. The firelight grew dim and a chill shot through my body.

"Excellent," he said. "We're quite pleased with your sentiment."

I looked around, but I didn't see anyone other than the old man. The sun had set making it easy enough to hide somewhere and bushwhack me. "My wife and son are dead, and nothing can change that fact."

"That's where your comprehension of this world, and the next, is lacking. There are certain," he waved his hand in the air, as if to catch a thought, "forces at work. Beings more than ready to help bring your family back from the happy hunting grounds."

I'd give anything to have her back, but what this man spoke of was impossible. Dead was dead, and that's all there was to the matter.

"Oh, Jeremiah, dead most certainly is not dead. That which is dead may eternal lie, but sometimes, that which is dead can be roused once again." Obadiah said, responding to words I thought I'd left unspoken. "We can bring them back, but at a price."

There was always a catch. Nothing in this life, or the next, was free it seemed.

"What's the price?"

Obadiah smiled.

"You'll have to carry something for us, something precious," he said.

If it meant getting my family, I could be an errand boy.

"Good," Obadiah said.

Before I could ask any questions, Obadiah reached into his coat and pulled out a leather pouch. The old man threw it at my feet.

"Go there, and look for the brujo," he said. "He can set you on your path and help get your family back."

I'd heard that word before, brujo. Some of the Mexicans would whisper the word under their breath while they made signs of the cross to protect themselves. Supposedly, they were shamans or witches of a sort. It didn't matter. If the brujo could bring my Sally back to me, I'd shake the devil's hand.

Obadiah continued to give me that rictus grin and nodded toward the pouch. I reached for it, but a sharp pain filled my head. Voices came alive, whispering horrible things in my ears. Again, the child's whimper of pain brought me back to the present.

"What is that, who's out there?" I asked.

My boots found the earth, and I was up in a flash, the hammer pulled back on my gun.

"Who's out there, old timer? Speak up!"

"Only the demons we bring with us," he answered.

"Don't you move."

I took a couple steps back then peered toward the wagon. With the fire burning low and the sun all but gone, it was difficult to see, but movement behind the wagon caught my eye. I just barely caught the sight of a coat behind one of the wheels.

"Come on out before I start shooting," I said.

There was a sharp intake of breath as someone scuttled back into the darkness. The child's cry slithered through my ears, and my gun wavered. I eased the hammer back into place. Then, I took a knee.

"It's okay, come out."

I stole a glance back at Obadiah. He hadn't moved from his perch on the log. He still wore that damned smile on his face, his head cocked to one side as if he were a mongrel dog. The man's coat shook as if buffeted by a howling wind, but the storm had died down to nothing. Movement from the wagon caught my ear, so I turned back to investigate.

A small hand appeared on the wagon wheel, followed by a head caked with mud.

"You come on out now, it's okay," I said, as gentle as I could.

A boy stepped out from the behind the wagon, wearing torn clothes stained with dirt and muck from the road. The boy shivered and hugged his chest to try and conserve body heat.

"Sam?"

As soon as I said his name, I knew it wasn't my boy. My heart lurched just the same as the memory of Sam playing in the mud puddle by the house came to me. He loved to get dirty and would take any opportunity to play in the muck.

I put the gun away and motioned him over with my hand. While I was half-frozen myself, the boy needed to get warm or he'd die. I took off my wool coat and offered it up. The boy took a nervous step forward but stopped. He started to cry. The tears cut muddy paths down his dirty cheeks.

I moved toward him, but he shied away, hiding behind the wagon again. I stopped and stood straight. As I stepped closer, it became clear. A rope tied around the boy's neck tethered him to the wagon. He clutched at the knot, but his cold hands couldn't loosen it from around his neck. Sam had tried to get the rope off his own neck, and I couldn't help him. At least I could save this child.

I drew my knife. The boy whimpered and tried to crawl under the wagon.

"It's okay, son, I'm here to help," I said.

I reached for him, and he started to shriek as if the devil himself grabbed at him. The old man's laughter picked up from behind me, and the two cries mixed together in an unholy sound. The child kicked and screamed and made it hard for me to get a clean angle at the rope.

I didn't want to scare him, but I needed to cut him free. The next time he lashed out, I caught his foot and pulled him out from under the wagon. His eyes were wide with fright, as if he'd seen a spook.

"You best just let that boy be, Jeremiah," the old man said, his voice somehow cutting through the child's wails to pierce my ears. "He can't help you like we can."

I ignored him. After I cut through the rope, I pulled the boy close to my chest. He fought for a moment but stopped when exhaustion took his body. Without a second thought, I started to hum an old lullaby I used to sing to Sam. I fell into the song like a bed after a hard day's work. The boy shivered against me crying but no longer fought to get away.

I brought him close to the fire hoping the flames would help warm his body. As we got closer, he started to twist away and kick.

"Calm down, it's okay," I said in the most soothing tone I could muster. It was too easy to fall back into being a father.

"No, no, no, no, no," the boy said over and over.

"What, what is it?" I asked.

He pointed across the fire. Obadiah no longer sat on the log but stood. He cast an imposing figure and seemed to tower above everything. The sick grin still called his face home, and I wanted nothing more than to wipe that smile away with a full serving of lead.

"It's okay, son, he won't hurt you. I promise," I said.

"You shouldn't make promises you can't keep, Jeremiah," Obadiah said. The old man took a step forward which sent the boy into a fervor. The child fought like a wild horse, but I held on tight.

"Don't you worry, I can keep this promise just fine," I said.

The man let out a grunt as he took another step forward. I backed up a step with my pistol free. The boy took the opportunity and broke away. He ran behind the wagon once again. What I saw stopped me in my tracks.

The moon had broken through some of the clouds and cast some light on the forest. The dark shapes of human bodies hanging from the mighty pines swayed in the breeze. From the looks of it, there were two adults and a child—the boy's family.

"Now leave the boy be. A man's gotta eat," Obadiah said.

I glanced toward the bacon in the fry pan. The old man's laughter crawled out his mouth and into my ears. Enough was enough. I spun back toward him and emptied the Peacemaker into his body. The shots echoed across the mountain as Obadiah fell over the log he sat on moments before. I took a second to reload my pistol then inched closer to where he lay.

I pulled the hammer back on the gun as I stepped over to the log, ready to finish the old man, but he was gone. His large capote was on the ground, but nothing more. I scanned the surrounding woods, but the old man was nowhere to be seen. Then something moved from inside the capote, a quick rustle. I aimed the gun, ready to deliver the final shot, when a deluge of small animals spilled forth from the coat. Raccoons, rabbits, badgers, martin, squirrels and many other types of critters ran from inside the coat and scattered into the darkness. There were more animals than should have fit from under that capote, but they continued to run out in a steady stream. The old man's laughter started again, from every direction. He laughed so loud it hurt, and I fell to my knees.

Then a hand touched my shoulder, and the noise disappeared. The boy stood by my side, wide-eyed and shivering. I took him into my arms and lifted him away from the capote. There were no more animals, but it didn't matter, we needed to leave.

"Come on, let's get out of here," I said.

The boy nodded and rested his head against my shoulder. As I walked toward my horse, my foot hit the leather pouch on the ground. I stared at it, unsure of what to do.

"Let's go," the boy said. His voice was too much like Sam's. If what the old man said was true, I could get them back.

I leaned over and picked up the bag. Inside was a folded piece of leather, although I couldn't tell what animal it came from. It was mostly hairless and very soft to the touch. A map was drawn on the leather. I'd lived most my life in these parts, so I knew where it pointed. A circle was drawn around the settlement of Canyon Shadows.

"Let's go, I'm hungry," the boy said.

I looked down at the child. Sam used to say the same thing. The boy's dark brown eyes cut through me. I smiled and put the leather pouch in my pocket. My fingertip caught on the edge of the daguerreotype and the metal bit into my skin. I pulled my hand out, stuck the finger in my mouth, and let the metallic drop of blood flow onto my tongue.

We mounted my horse and headed down the mountain, careful to pick our way through the moonlit forest. The rhythmic breathing of the boy told me he was asleep. I was dead tired and desperately needed sleep and food, but getting the child to a town where someone could take care of him proper was the first priority. Then, I'd find my way to Canyon Shadows and find the brujo. My mind was set, and the purpose gave life to the fires in my gut. The blood vengeance was over, but I realized now that killing those responsible was only a step towards this new, dark path—toward my family.

The sun peeked over the first mountaintop and drove some of the chill away. I closed my eyes and basked in the sun, hoping it would warm my bones. It was midday when we sauntered into a nearby town. It was a small farming community, so it wasn't hard to find a family willing to take the boy. They could use him in the fields when he grew a little older.

When I went to leave, the child ran to me and threw his arms around my leg. His grip was tight. Sam used to do the same whenever I would leave the house.

"It's okay, boy. These fine folks are going to take care of you."

He looked up at me with tear-filled eyes. The boy didn't have to say anything. I knew he wanted to stay with me. Hell, I saved him from some crazed thing in the woods, but the road wasn't a place for a kid his age. Plus, I had my own family to get back.

I peeled him off my leg and left him behind. He cried and tried to run after me, but the farmer's wife caught the boy and held him as I rode off. It was better this way.

The picture in my pocket gave me comfort, and the leather pouch beside it gave me hope. Hope that I'd once again have my family back, even if I had to go through Hell to get to them.

About the story: "The Demons We Bring" appeared in the anthology, *Old Scratch & Owl Hoots* published by Griffin Publishers back in January of 2015. This is a prequel to the story, "Horishi Tom" and shows where Jeremiah first found out about the demon's blood. I still plan on writing a final story about this character that bridges "The Demons We Bring" and "Horishi Tom" and what he has to go through to get the demon's blood. If you like the character, make sure you check out, *Alpha Protocol* which is the third book in my Dark Tyrant Series.

"Horishi Tom"

Utah Territories, 1867

The needle punctured skin and sent a flood of flame through my arm. Ice, colder than the northern winds, crept into my flesh behind that inferno. The freeze snuck in like one of Black Hawk's war parties. Funny thing, fire and ice mixing together slicker than stink on shit. All from that old bastard's needles. But I'm getting ahead of myself.

Name's Jeremiah Abraham Redford and I've been in hell.

Been living in it for over a year now. Ever since those sons of bitches killed my wife and little one. At least I think it's been a year. Time gets sloppy when you just don't care anymore.

Not saying I don't have motivation. Oh boy, let me tell you, I'm motivated enough. Just don't care about the little things. It's that cold motivation that brought me all the way to Anguish.

I pulled on the reins and stopped my horse. An old wooden sign stood near the side of the dust-covered road. *Stood* probably ain't the right word. The world tried its damnedest to bring that post to the ground. Yet, somehow, it still had the hard head to fight.

Deep-cut letters displayed the name *Angus* across the sign. Someone had painted an I and an H in big red print—Anguish. Fitting, I suppose. This town brought nothing but anguish to its inhabitants since the fire.

Unlike the sign, the town didn't fight to live. It gave up and died when the coal mines started burning deep underground. This town used to be a big deal. Angus fed coal up the rail lines on a regular basis. It was the black gold of the territories, and business boomed. I remember when I was just a kid, Papa brought me and my two brothers out there. First time I ever went to a big town. So many people and sounds.

Now, though, the town just lay in front of me like an empty shell. A skeleton dried up in the desert. Burned up and picked dry by the vultures.

Most of the vegetation, save for some of the hardier weeds, didn't last long around here. The burning coal underneath the ground poisoned the soil. My wife and her people used to stay away from Angus, said that constant burning invited evil things. She said Mother Earth was angry and refused to let anything grow. Didn't much matter anymore.

The daguerreotype in my pocket felt like it weighed a hundred pounds. Hell, the thin slice of metal didn't really weigh much, I suppose, but it always brought a heavy heart. I couldn't help but pull it out and look at it again--more a ritual now than anything else. But it hurt just as bad every time my gaze fell on those two faces.

My wife, everyone called her Sally because other folk couldn't pronounce her native name. It stuck after awhile. I used to get lost looking into those dark brown eyes easier than wandering through the southern canyons. She wore a nice new dress for the picture. Said it made her skin itch something terrible. I don't think she wore it again after that.

Then there was Samuel. My beautiful Samuel. Still trying to figure out how to walk straight. A miracle that we could get him to sit still long enough for the picture man to capture the image.

Both so wonderful. So wonderful and painful.

I stuffed the picture back into my pocket. The bent corner of the daguerreotype bit my finger as I pulled away. Memories hurt.

I wiped the finger on my coat and left a trail of dark blood. With a growl, I spurred my horse on. I wanted to get this over with. He whinnied in protest.

Damned thing had a heart just as stubborn as any ass I'd ever come across. Wouldn't budge no matter how hard I kicked or yelled.

I hopped off and hitched him to the sign. Figured if the post could fight the pull of the earth, then maybe it could fight the pull of the horse as well.

Before I entered the town, I grabbed the only thing valuable to me—a small leather pouch from the saddlebag. I needed the pouch, but that ungodly heat that rolled off it made my skin want to crawl right off my bones.

And the damned mumbling. The thing that rattled my teeth was that I could almost make out words in the mumbles. Could have been the wind, but I'd be liar if I didn't hear it anytime I handled that cursed thing. The quicker I could get rid of the bag, the better. Been nothing but trouble since I pulled it from that mountain.

I started to put the pouch in my pocket, but before I let go, I snatched it out and moved it to the other pocket. Didn't want that stuff anywhere near my wife and kid, even a picture of them. "Sorry about that, darlin'."

In the distance, the railway crept up and over the hill before stopping at a loading depot. The tracks sat on a raised mound of dirt, a snake of metal and wood that slithered off into the mountains. I hadn't seen it myself, but word was that not too much farther, the railroad company dismantled the track leading from town that connected to the main line. I suppose they didn't want to accidently send a car up this way.

The wind picked up when I took my first step into town. A warning? Who knows? I didn't care either way. I'd done too much and gone too far to turn away just because a Sunday breeze didn't agree with what was about to happen. I pulled my hat down tighter on my head, kept my eyes pointed toward the dirt, and made my way into Anguish.

Good Lord, now I'm even saying it. Anguish. Town's name is Angus. Just can't help but say it, though—rolls off the tongue too easy. Music to the ears in some sort of sick way.

Wooden and brick shops lined the streets like a bone orchard. They looked empty, but man alive, they felt occupied enough. Could've swore all those townspeople who just up and left sat behind those grimy windows and watched me as I marched up the road. Got the funny feeling they all stared as one thing, one mind. Of course, nothing stood behind those cracked windows. Nothing I could see anyway.

The smoldering coal fire had consumed most of the buildings. They lay in burned-out shambles, all charred wood and nightmare glimpses of what might have been a structure. More victims of Anguish, I suppose.

The only building with lights stood at the end of the path—the saloon. The townspeople had built it next to the mountain, nestled against the ginger rock of the cliff. The two-story saloon was imposing, like a bulwark to anything and everything.

The closer I got, the better I could read the large sign that decorated the front wall. Big, bold letters spelled *Billy Brock's Bar—Spirits and More*.

A pair of gas lamps guarded both sides of the saloon doors. Their dim yellow lights did little to fight the canyon's gloom, but in contrast to the rest of the town, they acted as a beacon.

I finally made it and my hands trembled as I pushed my way through the doors.

A sharp chill hit me in the gut. It stole my breath and ran with it.

A couple more gas lamps, as well as flickering candles in an iron candelabrum provided some light. It didn't help much, though, and the shadows danced about.

Tables with dusty glasses and overturned chairs littered the open room. A piano lay crippled and broken in the corner.

"Mr. Redford, the Horishi is expecting you."

I turned and drew my gun. I'm not sure what I expected, but I didn't expect to see a tattooed albino wearing a bowler hat pouring a drink from the bar. The man was taller than Big Hank from back home, and Big Hank had to duck whenever he came over to the house. The albino's skin was whiter than a brand-new bedsheet, and he had hair that looked almost transparent. Coal-black tattoos of serpents snaked all along the man's face and arms. He wore a button-up shirt the color of a moonlit night, sleeves rolled as far as he could get them. Rust-colored suspenders held a pair of black pants in place. I couldn't see all of him, but I suspected the tattoos ran all along his body.

Call me crazy, but the snakes seemed to move, always just out of the corner of my vision. It hurt to focus on them for too long.

"Who are you?" I kept the gun trained on him.

"I am the Assistant. I will help you with the transaction."

The Assistant had a funny way of speaking. It was hard to peg down, but he definitely wasn't a local boy. Almost sounded like one of them English folks, but there was something else to it.

"Where is he? I want to get this over with."

"Of course. I assume you have the required"—he circled his hand in the air a few times and took a long draft from his glass—"ingredient?"

I pulled the pouch from my pocket. The man's beady blue eyes narrowed, and his mouth twitched into a smile. He threw the glass against the wall and hopped over the bar. The Assistant moved quicker than I figured a man of his size would have been able to. I raised the gun and pulled the hammer back.

"That's close enough."

He stopped and put his hands out. This close, I could see the sweat bead up on his forehead. It ran down his face but avoided the snakes. He took a deep breath and put his hands behind his back. His gaze never left the small leather pouch.

"Of course. Please excuse me. I get excited sometimes. This way." He turned on his heel and marched toward a door near the back of the saloon. I lowered the gun, but followed him at a good enough distance in case he wanted to *get excited* again.

The door led to an old storeroom. Empty glass vials of all shapes and sizes littered the shelves. I clenched the pouch tighter and followed the Assistant down a set of stairs. I knew the layout. The stairs would lead to a cold room, a place they would have stored perishables. Yet as I followed him down, the air got thicker and hotter. Strange. Cold rooms were supposed to be cold. I wanted to shed my coat by the time we got to the bottom, but I didn't want to stop.

I was close now. Closer than ever to getting my family back.

"Is it true?" I asked.

The Assistant stopped at the threshold of another door. He turned and smiled. "Is what true, Mr. Redford?"

"Will this give me the power to bring the dead back to life?"

The Assistant looked away for a moment, but the smile never faltered. "You must work out the details with the Horishi." He opened the door and light spilled into the dark storeroom in a wave. I turned my head to the side and threw an arm over my eyes. Strange shapes danced behind my eyelids, shapes I couldn't explain. The same objects disappeared as my eyesight returned to normal.

Something cold touched my arm and I jerked away instinctively. The chill spread and I almost dropped my gun. The
Assistant stood next to me. He still wore that unnerving smile.
I rubbed my forearm against my pant leg to try and get some
of the warmth back, but it still felt as if I'd dipped it in lake
water in the middle of winter. I couldn't help but think one
of those damned snakes had slithered over my hand when he
touched it.

"Don't ever touch me again. You understand?" To stress my
point, I lifted the gun and pointed at his eye.

"My apologies, Mr. Redford, but the Horishi is waiting. He's
patient in his old age, but even his tolerance for tardiness has
its limits." The Assistant drew out the *s* in *limits*.

"Lead on."

The Assistant bowed slightly and walked through the door.
I followed him into the light-saturated room.

Hundreds of candles lined the walls on various shelves. The
display of light and shadow made me dizzy and sick. I choked
down a bit of bile that threatened to make an appearance and
sucked down some air. The scent of wildflowers hung in the
air, but behind that smell, the stink of rotting meat tainted the
room.

A small, old man wearing a dark red robe sat cross-legged
on the floor. Either the robes were too big or the man was
nothing but skin and bone, because he looked like a skeleton
in a sea of blood.

The old man pulled one arm out of the robe and let the
heavy fabric fall to the floor. Intricate tattoos covered his
shoulder and arm. They looked like picture-words the China-
men used to decorate their signs. The picture-words covered
almost every inch of the man's arm and shoulder.

He didn't have any hair on his head, maybe not even eye-
brows. I couldn't tell, though, because a white strip of cloth
covered his eyes. Black fluid soaked through the cloth where
his eyes should have been and trailed down his cheeks.

"Mr. Redford, may I introduce Horishi Tomo-sama," the Assistant said as he knelt next to the old man.

"Tomo Sam? Look, mister, can I just call you Tom?"

The Horishi smiled and revealed a bloody mouth devoid of teeth. He turned toward the Assistant and whispered something.

"The Horishi will allow it. He likes you."

The Horishi extended a gnarled hand, with his palm to the ceiling. I stared at it for a moment.

"The ingredient," the Assistant said.

I passed the pouch over to the old man. When he grabbed it, he latched on to my hand. Unlike the Assistant's cold, dead skin, the Horishi's burned hotter than coal in a stove. I wanted to pull away, but I couldn't. The old man had a grip stronger than wet rawhide. After a moment, the man let go and snatched the pouch from my grasp.

It was almost too much for me to handle. The town, the albino, and now this old man? Everything in my body screamed at me to leave. To turn tail and run until the sun rose. But that wouldn't get me any closer to my family. I focused on breathing to steady myself.

"A brujo down near the border told me you could help me bring my family back from the spirit world. That true?"

The Horishi opened the pouch. He pulled out a small glass vial filled with red liquid. When he popped the stopper and smelled the contents, his bloody grin grew wider than before. The Horishi whispered once again into the Assistant's ear.

The Assistant nodded and then stood. "The Horishi says that it can be done. He shall perform the rite and you will have the power to bring your family back. However, he wishes to know if you are aware of the consequences of your actions."

I'd heard what it would cost—my soul. But a little thing like that wouldn't get in the way of my family. They'd been taken too soon and I'd do anything to bring them back. "Yes, I know what I'm getting into. I agree to it. It's not for me. It's for my wife and child."

The old man said something, this time out loud. It was in a language I couldn't understand. His voice was just as cracked and aged as his body.

"What did he say?"

"He said that your hands are always welcome at the devil's washbasin."

The Assistant left me with Horishi Tom and shut the door behind him. The heavy sound of a lock sealed the deal. I was in it to the end now.

The old man pulled a shiny black box from inside his robe. Within was a small bowl and a piece of wood that had several sharpened needles fastened to the end. The Horishi poured the blood from the vial. It smoked and hissed as it hit the bowl.

He motioned me to him. I walked over and sat on the floor at his side. He grabbed my wrist once again. The familiar yet still-painful fire streamed up my arm. I gritted my teeth and tried to focus, but there was only flames. Then the old bastard spoke, and this time I understood.

"You and the demon will become one. Feed its desires, and it shall feed yours. Cross it, and it will dominate you."

I didn't know what to say, so I nodded.

The Horishi dipped the needles into the blood, rolled my shirtsleeve up, and we began. I don't know how long I sat there, but I felt every needle as it pierced my skin over and over. Each thrust brought with it the screams of my wife, the cries of my child. Their pain and suffering bored a hole through my soul and left it an empty husk. Tears ran down my cheeks as blood and ink ran down my arm. With each passing minute, the heat built up on my skin until I was sure it was going to bubble and melt away. Only one thought kept me still: my family.

The shadows on the wall danced in an endless hurrah as I sat in that room. Just as I thought I couldn't take any more, he stopped. The Horishi merely nodded toward my arm.

A simple design decorated my skin. A straight line ran from my wrist to the crook of my elbow. Circles crisscrossed the line and created the impression of a braid of rope bound together. The skin surrounding the tattoo was red and blistered. Yet that creeping sensation of ice throbbed in my bones.

"It's done?"

He nodded.

"My family, you can bring them back?"

The old man didn't answer this time; he merely bowed and turned his back to me. Instead, something else answered.

"Jeremiah, it's going to be a pleasure doing business with you. I'm sure we'll be such good friends."

"Who's there?"

A deep laugh rumbled through the walls of the building. Small waterfalls of dust fell from the ceiling as the thing chuckled. "I'm what you've been looking for, and you're what I've been looking for."

The voice crawled through my head like an earwig chewing its way to freedom. I clapped my hands over my ears but it didn't help. I'll be damned if the sound didn't come through clear as a church bell on Sunday morning.

Through the tumult, I still had one thought in my head and heart. "You can bring my family back to me?"

"I can do that. But you have to promise to play nice, Jeremiah." The shadows in the room seemed to flow into one spot on the wall. It wasn't long before the shadow took the shape of a man. "I can rip them out of the happy hunting grounds, but what are you going to do for me?"

I think I cried, but I couldn't tell. The thing's question echoed in my head. "Anything!"

The echoes stopped and the shadows ran back to their homes.

Screams cut through the air from the saloon upstairs. Screams that curdled my blood. Those cries took me back to when that group of cowards came to my farm. The same sound my wife made when the mob cut her apart like a beef cow. My son's wails edged into existence moments later.

"You're welcome, Jeremiah."

"You son of a bitch!"

My son's cries grew louder. I drew my gun and raced up the stairs. The Assistant was perched up on the bar and giggled when I burst through the door. He cocked his head to the side and stared at me.

Just as it promised, the demon brought my family back. Words have meaning, though, and phrasing's worth its weight in gold. The Assistant's giggles grew into a cackle as I stood there. I gripped my gun until my hand hurt.

My wife, my Sally looked at me with hate in her eyes. Rage and pain twisted her features until I could hardly recognize her. My poor son kicked his little legs and cried on the floor. They were just as I found them that day. Just as I found them after the mob had their way with them.

"Send them back."

Sally tried to crawl toward me but couldn't move well through the puddle of blood. She said something in her own language. I wasn't sure of all the words, but I knew enough to know when someone cussed at me.

"Send them back!"

Samuel coughed and shuddered. His cries cut me deeper than any knife could have.

"I'm sorry."

My hands trembled something awful as I pulled the hammer back on the gun. I barely heard the gunshots over the Assistant's laughter.

About the story: "Horishi Tom" is another one of my favorite stories. I had such a wonderful time mixing horror and western together. It appeared in Fictionvale's premier publication *Episode 1: Enter Fictionvale* in April of 2014. To date, this has been one of the only two short stories that I was paid professional rates for, and marks the highest grossing short story for me.

While I was writing the story, I wanted to do a re-telling of the Monkey's Paw, because I believe when you mess with dark forces there are always consequences. I wrote a prequel to this story, which appeared in the anthology, *Old Scratch & Owl Hoots* which gives the readers a glimpse of what pushed Jeremiah down the path towards damnation. At some point I plan on writing a story that will show the readers what happened when he met the brujo and how he obtained the vial of demon's blood.

If you keep up with my Dark Tyrant Series, you might have caught the easter egg I put in cross-referencing a certain Templar Knight from the novel, *Canyon Shadows*. Also, you'll see Jeremiah make an appearance in my book, *Alpha Protocol.*

"Kathy Loves Kittens"

The car slammed into our sedan with enough force that I think I blacked out for a few moments. When I came to, the world was spinning ass over end, and even though it was hard to focus, two things stood out. Kathy, my four-year-old daughter, shrieked in the seat behind mine, while my wife Olivia was eerily silent and calm.

Kathy's screams ended abruptly just before the car smashed into a large tree.

I tried to move, but the steering column pinned my body to the seat. My breath came in short gasps. I needed to check on Kathy, needed to know if she was okay. I thrashed against the seat and the steering wheel that crushed my chest but couldn't move the twisted metal.

In the distance, through the ringing in my ears and the metronome of the turn signal, the sad wail of sirens filled the air. They were slightly off tune and more akin to an air raid alarm than first responders. There was something else as well. A low mumbling, as if someone were muttering or giggling outside the car. Moments later, I passed out.

I awoke in a hospital room surrounded by the buzz of medical equipment and the steady beep of a heart rate monitor.

My entire body ached with even the slightest of movements causing me pain.

A woman walked into the room holding a clipboard. She wore a brilliant white medical coat and had her hair pulled up in a tight bun. Her eyes were soft, full of care as well as a hint of something else, something I couldn't place. Pain? Sadness?

"Mr. Devon, you're awake."

She said it with a hint of surprise, making a few notes on the clipboard. There was also something else behind her voice, something that matched the look in her eyes.

A nurse followed shortly after. He shot me an empty smile as he started checking my vitals. He was a squat fellow with a scraggly beard the color of a fire engine. Kathy loved fire engines.

"Where's Kathy?"

The doctor cocked her head, her eyes furrowed with confusion.

"Mr. Devon, how are you feeling?" she asked. "You've had a rough run, and you suffered a nasty blow to your head."

"Where is my family?"

She let out a sigh, pursing her lips.

"Mr. Devon, your wife is dead. Her funeral was two days ago. I'm very sorry for your loss. You've been in a coma for the last two weeks."

A mix of emotions ran through my mind. I was sad for sure, but empty more than anything else. I should have been a wreck, crying out against God and his decisions, but it wasn't in me. I was concerned about something else.

"What about Kathy?"

"Who?"

"My daughter."

I braced myself for the worst. Yet, I wasn't prepared for what she said.

"Mr. Devon, there was no one else at the scene of the accident other than you and your wife."

Kathy's bedroom was empty. Not just void of her presence but literally empty. Her furniture was gone. Her toys were gone. Even the damned poster of the kitten on the wall was gone. It didn't make any sense.

The police were less than helpful. All they had to offer were blanks stares, or even worse, looks filled with pity. The investigator in charge of my case, Detective Molly Shins, was nice enough, but she didn't believe anything I had to say about Kathy. No one believed me.

Kathy was real. I remembered when she was born at the Oak Heights Regional Hospital. Kathy entered the world peacefully, hardly making a noise. She was so small and warm against my chest, I never wanted to let her go. Going back to work those first few weeks after her birth was tough. Missing her first and second birthdays was tough. But I had to pay the bills. I had to provide.

I remembered her fourth birthday party. Olivia and I had gotten her a kitten, a little black thing with a white spot over one eye. Kathy loved that kitten so very much and named it Dr. Eyepatch. It was still here. It was real. It had to be because it nuzzled up to my legs as I walked by it in the hallway.

Olivia had kept a number of photo albums, which I thought was archaic. It was the digital age, but for whatever reason, she loved the look and feel of a physical picture. I grabbed one from under the bed and opened it.

Much like Kathy's room, all the photos of my little girl were gone. Blank spaces filled the albums, staring back at me as if holding little picket signs saying, *where'd she go? You don't know!*

My hands shook as I placed the photo album on the bed. It took me three tries to dial Detective Shins' number correctly.

"This is Detective Shins."

Her voice was a little raspy, as if she had smoked a pack a day for the last twenty years, but the few times I had actually been in the same room with her, she smelled of something bitter and sweet, not cigarette smoke.

"The photos are gone," I said.

"Mr. Devon?"

"The photos are gone. Just like the bedroom. Someone is—"

Shins' sigh cut me off, her patience was wearing thin.

"Grant, have you been taking the medication the doctor prescribed for you? Extreme trauma and a head injury can cause some *odd* things to happen," Shins said.

"God damn it, I'm not hallucinating! My daughter is gone—gone as if she never existed in the first place—and you and everyone else on the planet think I'm making it up."

The phone connection cracked and static leaked through. There was a rhythmic beep in the background followed by some unintelligible words. It didn't sound like Shins, even with her rasping voice.

"You're breaking up, Detective. I can't hear you." I checked my cell reception. It had full bars. As I returned the phone to my ear, Shins' sandpaper voice came through clear.

"I said I'll be by later to take a statement and check up on you."

It was out of pity that Shins was coming over, or to ensure I wasn't a danger to myself or anyone else. Her tone said it all, and her sigh told me more than I wanted to know. She'd be acting just the same as me, if not crazier, if it were her kid that was erased.

The doorbell rang, echoing through the empty house. Dr. Eyepatch scrambled past me racing towards the front door. I had barely hung up with Shins; there was no way she could have gotten here so quickly.

Whoever was at the door started to hit the bell faster and faster.

"Okay, okay, I'm coming," I said under my breath.

The doorbell continued to ring with a renewed fervor, the rings stringing together to the point that it almost turned into one long tone. I rounded the corner, and the front door was in sight. The ringing stopped.

Lightning crashed outside filling the darkened room with staccato light. It illuminated a figure on the front porch through the side glass on the door. The figure's shadow stretched across the walls, growing even taller.

The shadow disappeared as the lightning finished. I crept to the door, hesitant to open it.

"Hello?" I asked my throat dry.

There was no response.

Thunder rolled across the valley and shook the house. I sauntered up to the peephole and peered out.

The front porch was empty.

The wind blew the trees and shrubs around in a chaotic dance, and the lightning in the distance made it hard to focus, but there was no one out there. There was a low chuckle followed by incomprehensible whispers and mutters. I'd heard that voice before.

It was the same voice that came through the static on the phone. The same gibbering voice I had heard during the wreck.

"Who are you?"

Something slid across the porch, stopping just in front of the door. Another chuckle.

"Who are you?" I asked again, this time with more force. I looked through the peephole, trying to get a look at who was out there, but there was nothing but darkness and wind.

I twisted the doorknob and flung the door open with enough force that the knob left a hole in the drywall. There was nobody there. However, there was a cardboard box on the ground sealed with packing tape. Written in chicken-scratch handwriting across the top in black ink was a sentence that made me want to throw up. It read, *Kathy loves kittens.*

I pulled the box into the house and placed it on the kitchen table. For what seemed like hours, I stared at the box until finally I grabbed a knife from the counter and cut the packing tape. Hundreds of foam packing peanuts lined the inside, covering the contents. I rummaged around and pulled out a blood red envelope with silver filigree decorating the edges. My name printed with black ink in fine lettering adorned the front. A bulky wax seal with a red and black ribbon was on the back. On the seal was an impression of a crude, thin face with no eyes.

I broke the seal on the envelope and pulled the letter out.

Kathy loves kittens. You know this of course, but I find it quite amusing. She talks about Dr. Eyepatch constantly. Sometimes I think she wants to see the cat more than she wants to see you.

Who am I kidding? She adores you. Kathy refuses to go anywhere until she sees you again. That's the innocence of children, I suppose, still wanting to see you even when you mess up.

You messed up, Grant. While I want to give Kathy her wish, I'm not sure you deserve to see her. Let's see how much you want to find her. Listen closely and try not to get the song stuck in your head.

Regards,

-F.

My hands shook as I put the letter down, my head swimming with even more questions. I stood and went to the kitchen cupboard to pour myself a glass of whiskey. The alcohol burned on the way down and even worse on the way back up.

I'd never had that kind of reaction to alcohol before. Sure, there had been times in my younger years that I drank so much I threw up, but this was something else.

There was a muffled series of tones emanating from the box on the counter. I dug through the box, my hand brushing against a corner of something solid. I grabbed it and pulled it out, spilling packaging peanuts all over the floor.

It was a small short-wave radio. There was a knob for volume and an antenna. There were no brand markings or any lettering at all. The three tones sounded off again, louder now that it was out of the box.

I tried to tune the radio, but the knob refused to move. I adjusted the volume just as the three tones sounded off for a third time. This time, after the tones, music started playing. It was old, maybe from the twenties or thirties. Something that warbled a little, slightly off tune as it tried to be catchy. There was another noise. Something in the background of the music—a voice.

It was the voice of the person who had been at the wreck and stood outside my doorstep not moments before. He muttered a little and then laughed.

"Listen closely, boys and ghouls, we've got a special message for you today. Set your decoder rings to Hotel 03, kiddos. That's Hotel 03."

The music stopped, but there was still static.

Then Kathy's voice came on the air.

I fell to my knees, tears pouring down my face. Dr. Eyepatch floundered over to me, rubbing up against my hand. I scooped him up, holding him tight.

"She's alive."

Dr. Eyepatch let out a meow in response.

Kathy was still talking over the radio. I'd been so happy to hear her voice that I didn't even pay attention to what she said. I gave the transmission my full attention. I started to jot the numbers down on a nearby envelope.

"87456 87432 25346 88432 90331..."

Kathy droned on, spouting groups of five numbers. Her voice was flat and monotone, but at the end of the message, she giggled. I loved her giggle. It was so innocent and pure.

Then she was gone.

"No. Come back!"

I stood and grabbed the radio. I turned the volume up, but it didn't matter. She was gone.

"I hope you boys and ghouls got that super fun message. Tune in tomorrow for more. Don't lose your decoder rings, or you'll be out of luck, Chuck."

I dropped the radio.

I rubbed my head until it hurt. What could I do? Without the decoder ring, I wouldn't be able to make heads or tails of the message. I wouldn't be able to find my Kathy. I needed the decoder ring. I growled and flung the cardboard box off the table. Packaging peanuts flew across the floor in a miniature tsunami.

The doorbell rang, echoing through the house. Dr. Eyepatch poked his head around the corner then scrambled up the stairs.

I grabbed a knife from the knife block and stormed to the front door. If it was the guy who took my Kathy away, there would be hell to pay.

I flung the door open, knife at the ready, only to find Detective Shins' disapproving stare greeting me.

"Would you like to put the knife down, Mr. Devon?"

Shins looked at me from across my kitchen table then scanned the disaster that was the kitchen. She pursed her lips before writing something down in a small notebook.

"Can you describe the voice again, Mr. Devon?"

"It was deep and gravelly. Almost like someone who smoked a lot."

I glanced up to see if Shins would take offense to the smoking remark, but she continued to look at me with a blank stare.

"Do you have reason to believe that this person has anything against you, Mr. Devon? Someone you know, perhaps?"

"No, no one. I don't know who it is or why they are doing this, but they have my daughter."

Shins started writing again. She pointed to the radio on the table.

"This is device you found in the box?"

"That's correct."

Shins reached out for the radio but pulled her hand back before she touched it. Instead, she pulled out a camera and snapped a few photos.

"Mr. Devon, I'd like to ask you a few more questions about your wife."

I froze. I'd already answered too many questions about Olivia. "I don't see what Olivia has to do with my daughter's disappearance."

Shins wrote some notes down in her notebook and then looked at me. "Maybe nothing, maybe everything. It's my job to figure out the facts. Please describe the events leading up to the accident."

"I've already done this," I said.

"Humor me."

I stared off toward the liquor cabinet and my stomach churned.

"Mr. Devon, please answer my questions, and I'll look into this package as well as order increased patrols in your neighborhood. Perhaps your gibbering man will haunt your doorstep again."

"Why did you call him that?" I asked.

"Called who what?"

"The Gibbering Man? Why did you call him that?"

"I have no clue what you're talking about, Mr. Devon. Please stop avoiding the question."

The quicker I answered her questions, the quicker she would be out of here and searching for my daughter or this Gibbering Man. "We left the house around six in the evening."

"Where were you going?"

"I don't quite remember; all I know is that we were in a hurry."

Shins took some more notes. "Did you speed that night?"

"Nothing too crazy. Just the standard 5-7 miles over the limit."

"Did you mess up?"

You messed up, Grant.

"Excuse me?" I asked.

"I said, what did you and Olivia talk about during the ride?"

My stomach twisted, and I wanted to throw up again. Maybe I just needed a good night's sleep. I rubbed my forehead, but it didn't do much to help me focus. "I don't remember, small talk."

Shins nodded, jotted some notes, and then looked me in the eyes. "Did your wife make any phone calls prior to the accident?"

A small ache started in my knuckles and slithered up my arm. The metallic taste of pennies appeared in my mouth but was gone as quick as it came. "Not that I can think of, why?"

"We pulled your wife's phone records, yours as well. She made some interesting phone calls, Mr. Devon."

Shins gave me a devilish grin that spread ear from ear. This was the first time I remembered her ever smiling, and I didn't like it. I clenched my hand into a fist, and the ache in my knuckles turned into a burn. "What do you mean?"

Shins continued to grin at me, fire in her eyes as she pulled a folded piece of paper from her coat pocket. She took her sweet time unfolding it, knowing she was torturing me with each movement.

"You sure you want to know? Things change when you know things."

"What the hell is wrong with you?" I asked, slamming my hand onto the kitchen table.

Her smile disappeared, but the fire remained in her eyes. She left the paper on the table and got up. "I'll leave this here with you. Do what you want with it. Don't mess it up, Grant."

The room spun circles around me, and I stumbled to the kitchen sink, unloading round two of vomit. When I finished, Shins was gone, but the paper was still there.

I sat back down and turned it over. There was a list of Olivia's recent phone calls. I recognized my number, but she had also made a lot of calls to another number. I wasn't sure who it belonged to, so I called it.

It rang three times and then someone answered.

For a long time, there was nothing but heavy breathing on the other end of the line.

"Hello?" I asked.

"What do you want, Grant?"

I knew the voice. It belonged to my neighbor, Sterling Smithe.

I hung up the phone and flew out the door. Why the hell had Olivia called Sterling so much? I needed answers, and he had them.

He met me at the porch as I stormed up to his house. He had two black eyes and a bandage over his nose. That would explain the labored breathing.

I walked up to him, about to give him what for and ask the million-dollar question, when he socked me in the face.

I lost my vision for a moment when the world exploded. My ears rang, and blood filled my mouth. I tried to focus on him, but tears poured from my eyes.

He swung at me again, but I reacted in time, diverting the blow with my elbow as I brought my arm up to protect my face. I wrapped the same arm around his, hooking it tight, then I reared back and head-butted him in the face. Stars again, but this time he let out a cry of agony and dropped to his knees. I still had his arm hooked, so he dragged me to the ground with him.

"Enough!" Sterling said, holding his hands up as he rolled on to his back. "Jesus, Grant. I think you re-broke my nose again."

I touched my own nose and flinched.

"Pretty sure you broke mine, too."

I rolled away from him and got on my hands and knees. Blood poured from my nose, splattering his porch steps.

"What the hell was that about, anyway?" I asked.

"Give me a break. You get amnesia in the accident?"

I rubbed my forehead; it was tender where I had hit Sterling.

"Let's say I did," I said. I had a sneaking suspicion where this would go, but I had to play it through. "Humor me."

"Humor you? I ought to have you arrested. Last time you came over, you kicked the living shit out me. I get it, I probably deserved it, but you were a madman. If it weren't for Olivia, you would have killed me. I saw it in your eyes."

Sterling's eyes were wide as he talked. He kept his distance from me, jumping a little when I'd move.

"Damn... I can't remember any of it. Why did I attack you?" He spit out a thick wad of blood. "Seriously?"

I shrugged. I got to my feet and he scrambled back.

"Take it easy, I'm done. Just answer the fucking question."

He sighed and lay his head against his doorframe. Sterling covered his eyes, and it took me a moment to realize he was crying.

"Olivia," he said.

I knew it. She'd been a little too affectionate, a little too accommodating to my wants, as if she were making up for something. I was too busy or too stupid to realize it.

"You must have found out," he continued. "She called, warning me that you were coming. I was going to leave the house and let you cool down, but you got me before I could get in my car. You've got a mean right hand."

My knuckles tingled.

"But you messed up, didn't you, Grant?"

I looked up, and Sterling was smiling. Blood still poured from his broken nose, running down his cheeks and over his lips.

"You messed up and now she's dead!" He started laughing.

I lunged at him and hit him in the face so hard my shoulder jarred with the hit. Sterling's head snapped back into the door frame and he fell limp onto the porch.

I got to my feet and was about to turn to go back to the house when I noticed a picture in a silver frame sitting on Sterling's mantel. It was of him and Olivia.

I walked into his house and grabbed the picture. They were smiling sitting on a fallen pine tree somewhere in the mountains.

Rage boiled from my guts, and I threw the picture against the wall. The glass shattered and the frame broke. There was a small wad of paper stuffed behind the picture, just peeking out from one of the corners.

I grabbed it, careful not to cut myself on the broken glass. It was a bundle of papers consisting of post-it notes, notebook paper, and computer paper. Three haphazardly placed staples held them together. The front, written in crayon, stated: Secret Decoder Ring.

Sterling wasn't on the porch when I walked out of his house. I wondered where he had slunk off to, but I had bigger things on my mind. Things like the Secret Decoder Ring notebook I had found.

The notes I had taken on Kathy's numbers were still on the kitchen table. It sat next to Detective Shins' phone record.

I sat down and flipped open the decoder book. What was the key?

Hotel 03, boys and ghouls.

I found Hotel 03. The book was broken down into rows and columns, with the rows two digits and the columns three. Words, phrases, and numbers jumbled the pages. I grabbed the notes I had taken and started searching.

Dr. Eyepatch jumped up onto the kitchen table and about gave me a heart attack. He looked at the Secret Decoder Ring book and at my paper. He let out a short meow and then hopped off the table, running figure eights around my legs.

The first number I had written down was 87456. It took me a moment to figure it out, but the first two digits were the rows. The other three were for the column. I found it after flipping through a few pages.

I

I searched for the next number, 87432.

Want.

Then the next, 25346.

To.

I only had two left. I found the next.

Come.

Then the final one. My hands were shaking which made turning the pages hard. My nose still hurt like a sonofabitch, and my eyes were tearing up. I wasn't sure if it was from the broken nose or Kathy's message.

I found the last number and almost dropped the book. Instead of one word, it was an entire phrase.

...home, but I can't. I can't because you messed up, Daddy.

"What did I do? How did I mess up? I want to make it right!" I asked it to nobody, to everybody. What did I do that was so horrible that someone would take my little girl?

The shortwave radio kicked on, playing the old-timey music again. "That is the question, isn't it?" the Gibbering Man said over the air. "What *did* you do? Wish I could tell you, but I'm not allowed. Keep playing the game and hopefully you'll find out and make things right. This little girl wants to go home."

"Daddy?"

It was Kathy's voice.

"Don't worry, honey! Daddy is going to make things right! I'm going to get you and bring you home!"

The radio powered off.

I didn't know what to do. Shins was no help at all, in fact, I was starting to suspect maybe she was in on the whole thing. I grabbed the radio and headed upstairs to bed. I stopped at the top of the landing. Kathy's bedroom light was on.

"Hello?"

Dr. Eyepatch ran out of her room and down the hall.

I walked over to her room and peered in. It was as I had left it earlier, barren, with the exception of a picture on the wall. It was a poster of a kitten hanging on a tree limb with the caption of "Hang in There" in bold, white letters at the bottom. That damned poster, so cliché, but she loved it. It had been gone before, but now it had returned. I wanted to smile, but I didn't know what it all meant. Hang in there.

"I'm trying, Honey. I'm trying."

With nothing left to do, I went to bed.

I awoke in the middle of the night reaching out for Olivia. Her side of the bed was empty. Not new, but it still hurt to reach out and find her gone.

Dr. Eyepatch sat in the middle of the floor, staring at me. It was strange; he usually jumped up in bed. I flipped on the nightlight to get a better look.

He was sitting on another black and red envelope. My hands were shaking as I opened it.

The Gibbering Man, Grant? That's what you're calling me? I suppose it's better than what most folks call me. Kathy had fun reading that little radio message for me. Did you enjoy hearing her voice?

That was a treat just for you. Something to whet your whistle and get you motivated. Now here's the hard part, Grant. Read this next part closely and pay attention to the details. This isn't for you. You're exactly where I want you and nothing will change that. This is for Kathy. Tune in later for more instructions.

Tootles,

-F

Three tones blasted from the shortwave, echoing through the room. I grabbed a pen and paper from my nightstand and waited. The tones blasted again in a different rhythm, almost like the beep of hospital equipment.

It was getting harder to draw in air, and my vision started to tunnel, the color bleeding out until everything was a dulled version of itself. I dropped to my knees, the pen and paper falling to the floor. I tried to stand but only ended up pulling the blankets off the bed. There was a tremendous pressure on my chest as if the steering column still pinned me against the seat of our wrecked sedan.

The tones blasted one more time in a long, drawn out buzz...

Then, the music started to play. It was that same warbled tune from before, but with it, the pressure let off my chest. I took in one big gulp of air and the color returned to my vision.

"Welcome back, boys and ghouls, we've got another special message out there for you. This one goes out to all you fans of Ooey-Gooey Chocolate Chunk Extreme Cookies. There's truth in the center of those delicious devils. Now set your decoder rings to Papa 15. That's Papa 15."

I got my pen and paper ready, retrieving them from the floor. Would Kathy read the numbers again? To hear her voice was both elating and heartbreaking at the same time.

The static of the shortwave cracked, followed by the ruffling and rumble of somebody moving the microphone. Then, Kathy laughed.

It was the kind of pure laugh that only children could make, one that melted hearts and could paint a smile on the sourest of faces. It brought tears to my eyes.

"Hi, Daddy! I miss you. Say hi to Dr. Eyepatch for me."

"I miss you too, honey, stay strong for Daddy."

Someone whispered something in the background. It was *him*. I knew it had to be. His whispers crawled through the signal and into my ears, and I imagined I could hear his words. It was a jumble of psychotic madness that burrowed into my brain and burned red hot. The words themselves were never meant for human consumption, I knew this on some level of my psyche.

"Okay," Kathy said to the Gibbering Man, and the muttering stopped. "72105, 83222, 44357."

She repeated the numbers again, which was good. I had missed them the first time through. I was going over the numbers again when *his* voice bled through the radio.

"Don't mess up, Grant. Kathy's depending on you."

Then the radio went silent.

Dr. Eyepatch poked his head out from underneath the bed, giving me a look filled to the brim with boredom. He padded over to me and then hopped up onto the bed, sitting directly on top of my notes.

I scratched him underneath his chin, which elicited a soft purr from deep down in his kitty engine. After a moment, he grew bored of my affection and scampered off into the hallway.

I grabbed the notes and retrieved the codebook. Now that I knew how the messages worked, it didn't take long to decode. The numbers broke out to be one simple sentence.

I love cookies.

What the hell did that mean? What kind of message was it?

A blood drop splattered across the codebook, soaking into the white paper. Another one followed seconds later. I reached up to my face, and my fingers came away covered in blood.

I journeyed to the bathroom and flicked on the lights. As they flickered, I caught movement behind me.

It was Olivia. Her face was a collection of bruises and cuts.

"Why?" One word was all she said, but it cracked the bathroom mirror, breaking my image into two.

I spun around expecting her to be gone, as if this was some scene from a cliché horror flick, but she still stood there.

I'm not sure what was more disturbing, the fact that my dead, beaten wife stood in front of me asking why, or the fact that she smiled a cold heartless smile. Hate rolled off her like a stench and watered my eyes.

"Why did you mess up, Grant?"

"I... I didn't mess up, honey."

Her smile grew even wider, splitting her mouth into a bloody grin. Bits of flesh dropped from her cheeks and hit the floor, sizzling on impact like bacon in a hot pan. Smoke started to rise from her body, filling the bathroom with a sickly haze. The temperature shot up to sauna levels, and sweat began to bead on my skin. I turned to run.

Some unseen force slammed the bathroom door, nearly re-breaking my nose. I tried to open it, but it wouldn't open. The doorknob went red hot in my hands, searing the flesh.

"Why?" She stood behind me and screamed the question so loud my ears stopped working.

Since flight wasn't an option, I only had one avenue left—fight.

I turned, swinging with a wide haymaker. My fist connected with Olivia's head with a wild, glancing blow. She laughed, and even though my ears still rang, I could hear it clearly. I continued to hit her, smashing down with my fists and driving her to the floor. She laughed even louder.

"I didn't mess up, you did!"

Her face fell apart under my rain of blows until there was nothing left but a bloody mess on the bathroom floor.

I was sobbing, kneeling on the tile. My body shook, and I couldn't feel my hands. They were stained red, and I was pretty sure I'd broken a few bones.

The lights flickered again, and she was gone—disappeared as if she was never there to begin with. My hands were still broken and bloodied with the bathroom tile cracked from the repeated impacts. I found my way to my feet and looked in the mirror, expecting to see her again, but it was just an empty bathroom in an empty house.

I sank to the floor and curled up into a ball, hoping it was all a dream. Hoped that I would wake up and my family would be back, and everything would be right.

That thought train derailed when a large bang vibrated through the house, as if someone had dropped a bowling ball on the hardwood floor from two stories up. The lights went out with the crash, shrouding the house in darkness.

I got to my feet, feeling along the wall until I found the light switch. I flipped it a few times, but nothing happened.

I shuffled out of the bathroom. All the power was out, leaving the room nothing but a wall of black. I took a step but stopped when something ran through the hallway.

It was heavier than Dr. Eyepatch and had a different cadence.

"Hello?"

Nothing.

I moved with slow and deliberate steps toward the hall. My heart pounded against my chest ready to burst at any moment. The ringing in my ears wavered, coming in and out in a strange rhythm.

Something ran through the hall again close enough it brushed by my arm. It was cold, sending a chill up my arm and into my body. Whatever it was, it ran into Kathy's bedroom and slammed the door behind it.

"Who's there?"

Her bedroom light turned on, shining out from underneath the closed door like a beacon. Whoever was in there ran around the room in circles.

Then, there was a giggle. A child's giggle.

"Kathy? Honey?"

I ran toward the bedroom, flinging the door open. It slammed against the wall, rebounding back into my vision. Just before it cut off my sight, there was a blurred glimpse of a dark-haired child running past. It had to be Kathy.

I caught the swinging door and opened it fully, hoping to see my little girl playing in her room. But she wasn't there. Nobody was there. I checked back in the hallway to make sure someone didn't slip by, but I was alone.

The room was different than before. This time, Kathy's bed sat nestled in the corner made up with a fresh set of sheets. Her kitten poster still hung on the wall, but otherwise, everything else was gone.

I walked into the room and the overwhelming aroma of fresh baked cookies assaulted my senses. It was strong, as if this were Olivia's parents' house. They were always baking treats for Kathy. Her favorite was Grandma's Ooey-Gooey Chocolate Chunk Extreme...

I lowered my head against the wall. Of course! Everything pointed to the in-laws' house. We used to go once a month. Each time Kathy would get so excited because Grandma would let her help bake the cookies. I had to go there. As if in response to my idea, the houselights turned back on.

I returned to the bedroom and kneeled at my nightstand. There was a small gun safe secured to the inside. I punched in the correct sequence and the safe door popped open, but my gun was gone.

I searched all around the bedroom, but the gun and the ammo were missing. Time was running out. Kathy needed me, so I made a command decision and left without the weapon. I wasn't that great of a shot anyway.

I rushed down to the kitchen to get my car keys and found Detective Shins sitting at my kitchen table. Her gun was out and on the table.

She looked up at me with a tired smile, the kind people gave as almost an automatic reaction. Shins reached into her coat and pulled out a pack of cigarettes.

"You know, every time I smoke one of these things, it feels like my lungs are burning to ashes. But I can't stop."

I didn't know what to say, so I kept quiet. I couldn't take my eyes off her pistol. I took a couple of slow steps toward the kitchen counter where my keys were, hoping she would stay involved with her Don't Start Smoking advertisement.

"That's my penance, you see? Addiction drove me into the darkness, causing me to abandon everything. It wasn't just these little puppies, oh no. These were child's play. I went for the hard stuff." She rolled up her sleeve revealing track marks marring her skin like dozens of angry bug bites. From the corner of my eye her vein started to wriggle.

"Detective, is everything okay?"

She lit the cigarette and took a deep drag. Her face relaxed, and the inkling of a smile cracked her lips. Then, as quickly as it appeared, it disappeared, replaced by a grimace. Shins started to hack and cough until she spit up a wad of black blood on the kitchen table.

"No, Mr. Devon, everything is not okay. I messed up."

I inched closer to the car keys. If I could grab them and go, perhaps I could get out before she went nuclear. I didn't know what she was capable of, but the deadpan look in her tired eyes told me enough.

"I should have listened to her, took her seriously. But I was too concerned about my next fix to care. Maybe this all could have been avoided if I had just given a shit."

I stopped. "What are you talking about?"

She looked at me and took another drag of her cigarette. Her face contorted into a mask of pain, and she started hacking again, spraying the kitchen with more blood. When the fit passed, she put the cigarette out on the table, smashing it into the lacquered wood.

"I didn't care, and now they're dead. I messed up."

"Who's dead? Kathy? Do you know where she is?"

I took a step forward and Shins picked up the pistol, stopping my advance. I put my hands out in front of me.

"Whoa, hold on," I said.

"I know where your daughter is," Shins said. "She doesn't belong. She's there because you messed up."

She lifted the gun to her head and pulled the trigger. Brain matter, hair, and chunks of skull painted the fridge.

Shins slumped into the chair like a rag doll. Her eyes were open and staring at me, and I swore she still had that tired smile on her face. Smoke from the gunshot floated from her skull in a weak wisp, crawling toward the ceiling.

I wasn't sure what to do. I could call the police, but it would be a nightmare. More than likely they would want to take me in for questioning, and I couldn't afford the lost time. Kathy was depending on me to find her.

There was only one option, and that option was to move forward. I grabbed the keys off the counter and headed out the door.

I had to take Olivia's car because our other vehicle was totaled in the accident. It was a strange feeling. When I got in, I realized that I never drove her car anywhere. I had to adjust the seat and mirrors. When I turned the car on, her radio station buzzed to life, filling the vehicle with pop country music.

As I went to change the station, static came across the radio, drowning the song out and replacing it with *his* voice. "Hey there, boys and ghouls, you're burning daylight. Kathy doesn't have much longer."

The radio returned to normal; however, it wasn't playing the original song. Now it played Patsy Cline's "Crazy."

I took the message to heart and sped to Olivia's parents' house. I arrived to the sound of gunfire.

Two shots, with the living room window lighting up with the muzzle flash. I wish I had grabbed Shins' gun from her dead grip before I left, but my head hadn't been in the right place. Plus, how would I explain my fingerprints on the detective's gun when it all went to trial? It was bad enough that she was dead in my kitchen.

I killed the engine and got out of the vehicle. My brain screamed at me to get back in the car, drive away, and call the cops. Let them handle the attacker. Yet, my heart—the heart that yearned to see Kathy safe—demanded that I go inside.

I crept up to the door, trying to be as quiet as possible. I stopped on the porch and listened, hoping to catch some indication as to how many people were in there or if they were moving around; however, there was nothing but crickets and the low hoot of an owl in the nearby cottonwood trees.

As I reached out for the doorknob, I had an eerie sense I'd been there before in that exact moment. I tried to shrug the feeling off but stopped when I turned the knob, placing my opposite hand on the door. There was a bloody handprint right where I'd put my hand. The dimensions fit so perfectly that I pulled away and inspected my fingers for blood. They were clean, as far as I could tell, but something was wrong.

In my mind, I already knew how this was going to play out. I would enter through the foyer and the lamp would be overturned as well as the shoe rack.

I opened the door, and sure enough, just as I thought, it matched my memory completely.

I didn't know what it meant, but it couldn't mean anything good. Next, I would turn the corner, and Olivia's parents would be dead on the floor, lying in a pool of sticky blood.

I still hadn't heard any movement, but deep down, I knew there wouldn't be any. This was becoming too familiar, and I knew what the end result would be.

I took a deep breath and rounded the corner.

There were two pools of blood but no bodies.

The coffee table was on its side, and their old Jurassic-era CRT television was face down on the floor. The smoky, metallic smell of a fired gun permeated the air so thick I could taste it. I backed out of the living room, almost tripping over the overturned coffee table, all the while reeling from the intense feeling of déjà vu.

Something chimed from the kitchen. It beeped in a rhythm following the beat of my heart before turning into a mechanical cadence.

"Hello? Is someone there?"

The beeps sounded again. I moved to the edge of the kitchen entryway and peeked in. The lights were on, but nobody was in there. The beeps were coming from the oven. It was the cooking timer.

I approached the oven, cautious as to what I might find in there. Reaching out with a shaky hand, I turned the timer off just as it started to sound again. I peered through the little rectangular window, hoping to get an idea of what was baking, but couldn't see through the gloom. Rather than turn on the oven light, I opted to open the door.

The mind-blowing aroma of freshly baked cookies rushed out into the kitchen followed by the blast of heat from the oven. The heat rolled over my skin, which at first was nice. I didn't realize how cold I was until I opened the oven, but the pleasure soon faded. It was hot, too hot for comfort and worse than it should have been. For half a moment, I thought my skin would ignite right there in the kitchen and I would be engulfed in an inferno.

I backed away, running into the table. It scooted across the linoleum sending a low rumble through the house.

"Grant, what's wrong with you? Shut the door."

It was Olivia's mother, Patricia.

I turned to face her, and my sanity fractured ever so slightly. She stood in the entryway between the living room and the kitchen. Her face was a mess of blood and bone. Whoever had shot her shot her in the back of the head, and the bullet exited through her eye socket. The exit wound was enormous, big enough to see through. The bullet had obliterated her nose and half of her cheek hung to the side as if it were a piece of deli meat.

"Jesus Christ."

"Language, young man," Olivia's father, Morgan said, although it came out in a mumble. I turned and found him standing in the other entryway leading out to the hall. Similar to Patricia, he had been shot in the back of the head, but for him the bullet had gone through his lower face. His jaw hung at an odd angle, touching his chest. Blood oozed out in a line of drool onto the floor, followed by the quiet clink of a tooth.

"Morgan, now we'll have to clean up the floor," Patricia said.

"This can't be happening, this isn't real," I said.

"You're right, it isn't happening. It happened," Morgan mumbled.

"It happened because you messed up," Patricia said.

They both walked into the living room and each lay down over their respective blood pool. Patricia propped up on her elbows and looked up at me. The light from the kitchen caught her eyes and they took on a shine not unlike a cat's in the dark.

"Please turn off the oven before you go," she said. Then she fell face first onto the living room floor, dead. A woman's scream cut through the house, rattling the foundation and causing the lights to flicker. It seemed to come from everywhere, and I couldn't shut it out no matter how hard I plugged my ears.

I left without turning off the oven, stumbling through the living room, doing my best to avoid Olivia's dead parents. As I exited the house, another gunshot barked, this time from the upper level of the house, and the screaming stopped.

I fished in my pockets for the car keys when I noticed Olivia's car was gone. Instead, my sedan sat in the driveway. It was just as I remembered it before the crash, as if nothing had happened at all.

I rubbed my eyes, hoping it was a trick or illusion, but it was still there. The world tilted and turned, causing me to throw up in the nearby lilac bushes. My heartbeat skyrocketed, and for a moment, my vision blurred.

My body spasmed as if I'd just stuck a butter knife into an electrical outlet, and I dropped to the ground in a heap. I tried to get up, but it hit me again, and I dropped to the concrete unable to breathe.

I couldn't see, and all around there were voices. The words were jumbled, and I couldn't make a lick of sense of anything. Yet, through it all, *his* voice came through above all else. The constant gibbering of something just beyond understanding, as if all I needed were a final piece of the puzzle and it would all make sense.

My vision came back slowly, blurry at first. I rolled to my stomach and pushed up until I could get my knees underneath my body. I sat back and took in a deep lungful of air, relishing the oxygen. My sedan still sat where Olivia's was a moment before. The door was open, with the constant chime letting me know it was, in fact, open with the keys in the ignition.

When I felt ready, I stumbled to the car and got in. Everything was as I had left it, to include my revolver wedged between the driver's side seat and the center console. I vaguely remembered putting the gun in my vehicle, but I couldn't quite remember the reason.

I picked it up, opening the cylinder. There were three spent shells with two ready to go.

The radio chimed on, three tones blasting indicating another message was incoming. I searched around the car, looking for something to write with. That's when the Gibbering Man came over the air.

"Howdy, boys and ghouls. I hope you've liked our little show so far. We're nearing the end of our spine-tingling tale of terror. Stay tuned, because who knows what might happen. Turn your decoder rings to Lima 03. That's Lima 03."

The old-timey music played again, giving me a chance to dig a pen out of the glove box. I didn't have any clear paper, so I used my vehicle registration. The music stopped, and I waited.

"Daddy? Are you there? I want to see Mommy now. I don't like it here anymore."

Kathy was on the verge of tears. I'd heard her like this hundreds of times before.

"I'm here, honey. Stay strong, Daddy's coming."

The Gibbering Man mumbled something quiet in the background.

"Okay," Kathy said. "But then I want to see my mommy."

More incoherent ramblings.

"34505, 40423, 76233, 22893, 19203, 68754."

I scribbled the numbers down, and the radio went silent. I dug the codebook out of my pocket, looking up the coded message.

Daddy

Why

Did

You

I knew what was next. It hit me from deep down, and I said the words before I wrote them.

"...hurt Mommy?"

I hadn't hurt Mommy. Yet, even as the thought crossed my mind, my knuckles ached, and I couldn't stop looking at the pistol.

It couldn't be. There was no way.

"Really, Grant? No way?" Olivia said from the passenger seat.

I looked over to her and wished I hadn't. Like her parents, she had been shot. A bullet hole was centered on her forehead with a steady stream of dark blood pouring down between her eyes. It ran in a channel around her nose and into her mouth. When she spoke, it sprayed all over the interior of the car, sprinkling me in the face.

"Olivia? What happened?"

I knew what happened. The knowledge was there. It was always there, just under the surface. But I needed to hear it.

"You happened. You messed up."

She reached across and placed a hand on mine. It was hot and I wanted to pull away, but I couldn't.

"Leave me alone!"

She smiled and squeezed my hand, sending waves of pain up my arm. My chest constricted, my heart missing a beat. I tried to breathe, but my lungs refused to cooperate.

"I wish I could, honey buns, but I'm not leaving without Kathy. She's home now, playing with Dr. Eyepatch. Let her go," Olivia said. She still wore a smile on her face, but her voice was ice cold.

She let go of my hand and slumped into the seat, dead. As soon as she let go, my lungs started to function again and the pain in my chest dissipated. For a few moments, I sat there taking deep breaths, never taking my eyes off my dead wife.

How could I let Kathy go if I hadn't even found her yet? Besides, if she thought I was going to give up my daughter to her, she had another thing coming.

Olivia mentioned Kathy was home. I didn't know what to believe anymore, but I'd run out of options. I threw the car into reverse and pulled out of the driveway. Kicking it into drive, I buried the pedal and raced back toward the house.

Olivia still sat lifeless in the passenger seat, and I kept stealing glances her way, worried she would spring to life and grab me again.

Something moved in the back seat. Instinctively I looked at the rear view, expecting to see Kathy back there playing with one of Olivia's health magazines. However, it wasn't her. It was *him.*

A man sat in the back seat wearing a dark suit and a tan colored trench coat. He was tall, having to lean forward to fit. It wasn't that he appeared out of nowhere that almost caused me to swerve off the road, it was his face. His nose was too long and hooked like a hawk's beak, and his cheeks were very distinct, as if chiseled from stone. He pulled his mouth into a wide grin showing rows of long, crooked teeth ending in deadly points. The most disturbing thing was his lack of eyes. He didn't even have sockets, just smooth skin where they should have been.

He opened his mouth, and static spewed forth. The radio in the car turned on, mimicking the same static. It turned louder and louder until I thought my brain would burst. Then came the gibbering.

Thousands of voices were talking, whispering, laughing, and screaming. The screams were the worst—millions of tortured souls crying out for it all to stop. Then he closed his mouth with a snap and cocked his head to the side. His voice came through the radio.

"We're almost at the end of our ride, boys and ghouls. We're coming to a crossroads. Time to make a choice."

"What do you want?"

"I want Kathy to be happy. Isn't that what you want?"

I mashed the gas pedal once again, accelerating. Trying my damnedest to be subtle, I reached down and grabbed the pistol. There were still three shots. More than enough to spread this *thing's* brains all over the backseat.

"I can make her happy."

"Let's be real. You haven't done a bang-up job yet, have you?"

A kaleidoscope of memories slammed my mind. Memories of me ignoring Kathy and leaving Olivia to deal with her. Memories of me yelling at my daughter, leaving her in tears.

I'd beaten Sterling Smithe nearly to death when I had found out about him and Olivia. Then I'd gone after her. I remembered attacking her in our bathroom, beating her nearly to death. She'd taken Kathy and ran off to her parents' house. Then came the drinking. That's what sealed the deal and set my mind to the task. I was going to make things right and make sure that we were all happy, but I messed up.

I drove to her parents' house, broke in and killed them, shooting them execution style in the living room. Then I killed Olivia in the upstairs bedroom. I dragged her body to the car, collected my daughter, and hit the road. She was in the backseat crying. I wanted to make her happy and stop her tears. I wanted all of us to be together again, one big happy family.

I was trying to calm her just before we wrecked.

"I'm so sorry," I said to no one in particular.

"You will be. But like I said before. This isn't about you. It's about her."

"Kathy?"

"Bingo! She's stuck, and you need to let her go. This isn't the place for her."

Her voice came across the radio.

"Mommy? Is that you?"

Olivia was no longer in the front seat of the car.

"Yes, Pumpkin, it's me."

They were both crying, and I could picture them together, holding each other in a tight embrace.

"I can make it work. I can make it better," I said.

"I'm afraid we're past that point. But if you don't let her go, she'll be stuck here with you."

"Let her go," Olivia said.

Once again, my chest constricted, and I couldn't breathe. This time it was worse. An intense pressure mounted in my shoulder, and I slumped forward in my seat.

I just wanted them to be happy, no matter the cost. It was the last thing I remembered before my car slammed into another sedan that looked eerily just like mine.

I wake up in a hospital room with the mechanical buzz of medical equipment and the steady beep of a heart rate monitor. The window shades are pulled, but the warm summer sun bakes outside the window.

I look around the room, but nobody is there.

I open my mouth to speak, but my throat is incredibly parched, and I can't make anything more than a half-hearted hacking noise.

I try to get up.

"Kathy?"

It comes out more like a croak than a word, but it got someone's attention. A woman walks into the room holding a clipboard. She is wearing lavender scrubs and a medical mask over her nose and mouth. Her eyes are hard, and specks of blood coat the front of her outfit.

"Mr. Devon, you're awake." She says it with a hint of surprise, making a few notes on the clipboard. A nurse follows her in. He's a big fellow with tattoos running down both forearms. He gives me a sneer as he begins to check my vitals.

"Where's Kathy?"

The woman lowers her head a bit, avoiding eye contact.

"Mr. Devon, how are you feeling?" she asks. "You've had a rough run and we've had to bring you back a few times. We weren't sure if you would make it."

"Where is my family?"

She lets out a sigh and pulls the mask from her face.

"Mr. Devon, your wife is dead. Her funeral was two days ago. You've been in a coma for the last two weeks."

I lean my head back and shut my eyes. This wasn't what was supposed to happen. I was supposed to bring us back together and make us a happy family.

"And my daughter?"

"Mr. Devon, your daughter passed away minutes ago. She died in surgery."

I want to say something, but I can't, all that comes out is a low wail. I need to see her one last time before she's gone. I want to get up, but that's when I notice my arm is handcuffed to the hospital bed.

"Let me out of here. I need to see her. I need to see my daughter!"

I struggle against the bonds, thrashing in my hospital bed. The woman whispers something to the nurse, and he nods, running out of the room. Moments later, Detective Shins walks in. Her eyes have a glaze over them as if she's riding a high and not quite with it all. Whenever she looks at me, her face conveys guilt. Another detective accompanies her. He's a tall man with a hawkish nose and deadpan eyes.

"Mr. Devon, we're glad to see you're awake. We have some questions for you regarding the death of your wife, Olivia."

I sink back into my bed and can't help but laugh. I know what waits for me when I die. I've tasted Hell and it's inside me now. I know *who* waits for me when I die, and it isn't Kathy. It's the *Gibbering Man*.

About the story: "Kathy Loves Kittens" deals with one of my biggest fears—losing a child. I originally wrote this story for an anthology dealing with haunted signals. It made it through the slush but couldn't quite make it to the finish line. The problem was, it was a long story, as the call for submissions gave me latitude to expand on it. This meant it was a hard sell for other open calls for anthologies, as the normal range you see is max 5-6k words and this story originally clocked in at 12.5k words. I later trimmed it down to 10k and it was picked up by Tales to Terrify and turned into an audio podcast. If you want, you can listen to it.

About the Author

C.R. Langille spent many a Saturday afternoon watching monster movies with their mother. It wasn't long before they started crafting nightmares to share with their readers. They are a retired, disabled veteran with a deep love for weird and creepy tales. This prompted them to form Timber Ghost Press in January of 2021. They are an affiliate member of the Horror Writer's Association, a member of the League of Utah Writers, and they received their MFA: Writing Popular Fiction from Seton Hill University.

Follow their exploits at: https://biolinks.heropost.io/CRLang ille

If you enjoyed this story, please drop me a review. Also, check out some of my other stories as well. Finally, subscribe to my newsletter and never miss out on new releases, book/movie reviews, and fun survival tips. http://www.crlangille.com/inbetween-newsletter.html

If you enjoyed, *Tales from the Storm*, please consider leaving a review on Amazon or Goodreads. Reviews help the author and the press.

If you go to www.timberghostpress.com you can sign up for our newsletter so you can stay up-to-date on all our upcoming titles, plus you'll get informed of new horror flash fiction and poetry featured on our site monthly.

Take care and thanks for reading, *Tales from the Storm* by C.R. Langille.

-Timber Ghost Press